WHEN LIGHT BECAME A MAN

BY

JOSEPH A. WAILES

OUTLAW PRESS
RAWHIDE, TEXAS

ISBN 978-0-9916454-1-1
PRINTED AND BOUND IN
THE UNITED STATES OF AMERICA

OUTLAW PRESS
2980 PHYLLIS LANE
RAWHIDE, TEXAS
75234-6425

THE WINNER OF THE HUMAN RACE

BY
JOSEPH A. WAILES

BOOKS AVAILABLE AT OUTLAW PRESS

TABLE OF CONTENTS

DEDICATION

This work is dedicated to the glory of the Father, the Son, and the Holy Spirit.

Also worthy of honorable mention are my Dad, Joseph Gorton Wailes, and my Mom, Aleene Anderson Wailes. They were very mighty witnesses for the Lord, and they introduced me to Jesus at an early age. They spent their whole lives in this world faithfully living out a sincere Christian life, and did it at home, too, behind closed doors. They proved to me that God is good.

FOREWORD

Many of us grow up very blessed, indeed, to have Christian parents, who teach us the things of the Lord. If they are sincere about it, they also live it out faithfully, year after year. We have a definite head start on the pathway to find Jesus. I was taught to read at an early age, and loved to read the Word of God. Also, among my favorites were Sir Arthur Conan Doyle's famous stories of Sherlock Holmes. I developed a taste for adventure stories, too, like the tales of King Arthur, and J.R.R. Tolkien's books about Middle Earth, as well as works by C.S. Lewis. I had a keen interest in science, and also science fiction. I was taught to follow the evidence, but be led by faith. As the Scripture reads, "Oh, taste and see that the Lord is good!"

Ronald Reagan also said something about, "trust, but verify."

My various experiences throughout life
have proven to me, beyond reasonable
doubt, that the Word of God is absolutely
true, and the Name of God is absolutely
Holy, and the Spirit of God is absolute
power. One of the purposes of this book
is to spark some curiosity on the part of
the reader, to perhaps even motivate
someone to actually open their Bibles,
and see if any of these notions have any
validity. If you find errors, well, please
understand, I did my best to check all the
cross references, connections, and
interwoven threads which I was honored
to be allowed to follow through
Scripture, from Genesis, to Revelation.
Any errors you find are honest mistakes,
or misunderstandings, on my part, so do
not blame God, if I wrote it down wrong.
I hope you will approach these ideas with
an open mind, and at least consider if
such things might actually be the case in
reality, seen, or unseen. This is not
science-fiction, or sci-fi. Rather, it is

Scripture-based-fiction, maybe call it Scri-fi? As I suggested, if you think my idea is all wrong, look all of the elements up in your Bible, and see for yourself. Stop taking someone else's interpretation of the Word of God as though it is Gospel, unless you read it for yourself, and find out what it really says. Pray about it, and our Lord will help you understand some of it, but not all. Nobody but Jesus understands the whole Bible.

THE LITTLE GRAY DONKEY

There happened a brilliant morning in the great meadow one day. All the King's horses were eating or playing, running free and thoroughly happy, as they chased each other, as colts often will. Every one of them was strong and fit, in excellent condition.

Suddenly, a piercing whistle cut through the air. Every horse stopped and turned toward the sound.

A mighty voice rang out, "Today is the Day!"

All the horses immediately ran at full gallop toward the voice. As they came near, they saw a Man, dressed in shining white armor, so bright it overcame the eyes. His eyes were like living flames, and no one could meet His stare. His face was strong and kind, full of joy. Every horse dropped to knees, and bowed before the King. They all waited quietly, as He walked briskly through the midst of them. He kept walking for several minutes until He had come to the very back of the mighty herd, over a million strong. He stopped when He reached a little gray donkey at the very utmost back of all the other proud warhorses.

He smiled, and said, "Stand up, little friend! This is the time foretold for ages, and this is the Day! I ask you to carry Me once more, as you did 2,000 years ago, the day we rode into Jerusalem, and stormed the devil's stronghold."

The little donkey lifted up his eyes, and slowly stood up. As he did, he began to grow larger and much more muscular, much longer-limbed, and greater in strength and ferocious appearance. As he finished standing, no longer gray, but glowing a dazzling bright white, he had suddenly become the largest and most fearsome of all horses ever, and threw back his mighty, noble head, and sent out a deafening challenge that shook the ground. All the other horses also stood, and echoed his call.

The King leapt upon His enormous steed, and sent out His own shout that shook even the fabric of the air as an earthquake! All His other riders also echoed His mighty war cry, as they each leapt upon their own mounts. They parted a space for the King to ride through, and, as He reached the exit from the great meadow, every voice, man and horse alike, lifted as one and shouted, "Holy, Holy, Holy!" as they followed the King into battle!

STAR WITHOUT LIGHT

When it hit, it penetrated the tectonic layer like an armor-piercing bullet. It bored deep into the heart of the planet, carving a hole hundreds of miles wide, and thousands of miles deep, edges crisp like a giant laser had cut them. As it met dense magma, it slowed dramatically until it stopped near the center.

Back at the surface, a huge patch of water the size of Australia had instantly vaporized, and a mushroom cloud three thousand miles in diameter rocketed upward into space. A mega wave seventeen miles tall and two hundred miles in duration raced outward at near the speed of sound, expanding in all directions.

The tectonic layer shattered into many distinct large plates, most of them ontinent sized. The shockwave travele ugh the structure of the Earth,

making permanent changes. The single
giant continent on the opposite side of the
globe from the impact, Pangaea,
immediately split from top to bottom,
with about thirty five percent beginning
to drift westward, and the rest beginning
to drift eastward, as the enormous section
of tectonic plate under the super
continent split into several pieces and
spread apart. At not only the impact site,
but also at every split in the tectonic
layer, columns of molten rock shot miles
into the sky, and flowed all over the
ocean floor, where in water, and across
the land, if not near water initially, before
the ocean rushed into the new cracks.
Steam began to cover the Earth, and it
started to grow dark, except for the fire of
vegetation burning, worldwide, and the
burning magma spewing out.

The initial impact site was thrust
upward from the shockwave echo, and
the release of the magma. This feature

later became known as Hawaii. This series of spectacular events was not all.

All those things could be observed upon the planet's surface, or atmosphere. But inside, under miles of rock, the collapsed star did not remain at rest, but began circling the Earth's center, establishing a mutual center of gravity, slightly off-center, tilting the earth on it's axis about 23 degrees, causing a wobble to the revolutions, generating a magnetic field, where one had never been before, and from then on, causing an endless series of seemingly random volcanic eruptions, landslides, formations of mountain ranges, canyons, and ocean floor trenches.

The small planet which the burnout had been dragging along with it had assumed a new, very stable orbit around the new star-within-a-planet combination, and soon was even tidally locked into the gravity field. But there was one effect that was even observable from our nearest neighbor star, Alpha Centauri, four light years distant. Four years after the impact, a momentary flash, brighter than the sun, could be seen from earth. It was the last time ever that the fallen dark star had anything to do with light. It spent the rest of forever in darkness.

THE SONS OF NOAH

Fourteen years had passed since the waters had drained away. As the huge flood had ended, the world's rivers formed great mud carving machines that gouged out features like the Grand Canyon from the saturated and softened earth. The young men were very restless, hungry to go explore the freshly washed world, cleansed from the evil which had been choking the life out of it.

Within the first year after the flood, they had all relocated down from the summit of Ararat, leaving the Ark intact, wedged between the rocks where it had come to rest. The world's climate was beginning to stabilize again, and snow and ice were beginning to cover the mountain, and even starting to frost over the Ark. All of the animals had wandered off within weeks, as soon as the level of water dropped sufficiently to allow travel. Of course, the men had retained a few of the farm type animals, so they could have milk and eggs, and so forth.

Noah was beginning to feel his age. After all he was nearly one hundred and forty years old. As a young man, he had heard the Lord, and begun work on the ark, which had taken him and his sons over a hundred years to build. Part of the time had also been spent gathering all the different classes of animals, collecting only the strongest and fittest of them all, so they could help after the flood to repopulate the world. He had blessed his sons after the flood, and assigned each one of them his own direction of travel for their futures. Shem, his firstborn, he had commanded to go due south, into the most fertile and lush region available, the ancient middle east and Mediterranean area. Japheth, his second born, he had ordered east, into Asia. His youngest, Ham, had been told to head west into another very advantageous area, all the lands north of the Mediterranean. Ham had always been stubborn and wayward, though, and had instead decided to head south, and maybe see if his oldest brother, Shem, would give up part of his own vast area to him, and Ham wanted that very much, not because he cared to be near his brother, but he envied the lushness of the land, and the very mild winters there. This produced a great conflict between Shem and Ham, because Shem was not about not surrender even one square inch of his birthright from their father. Shem realized that doing that would have been disobedience, and rebellion, and so he would not agree with foolish Ham in his wickedness. Instead he drove Ham away from him to the west, warning him not to ever return, upon pain of death. Ham still was too stubborn to head back to Europe and its' winters, so instead he ran southwestward, down into unsettled Africa. Over the following centuries, God blessed all of the sons, and they swelled into entire stocks of the human race, each stock bearing forever the distinct family resemblance to their forefathers. Three forefathers became three stocks of mankind. Over time, the descendants of Shem filled the fertile land, and overflowed northward and westward, since Ham's descendants were not there in Europe. The descendants of Japheth filled all of Asia, and became very great also.

The descendants of Ham indeed did fill Africa, but retained an isolated existence for the most part, unwilling to trade and interact with the other regions and peoples. They seemed content to hunt the strange beasts in that land, and live off the abundant vegetation which also fed them well enough. As the millennia flowed by, the rift in the branches of Noah's family became even more pronounced, until Ham's people were seldom encountered or known in the rest of the world, which was busy building nations, and fighting great wars to control everything around them.

It did not begin to happen until the final few centuries of time in the history of earth that the far flung long lost cousins began to reestablish communication and trade. Once modern travel and contact had occurred, the world at last was becoming re-united. It should have been a happy time, but all the branches had grown so far apart, that they seemed as aliens from other planets to each other, and in some ways, that is exactly what they had each become. Every culture had developed its' own attitudes and ways of life, and no one was really eager to change what they had done for so long.

The Heavenly Father turned to His Son and said, "Even though they have forgotten that they are literally all of the same blood, those who are saved will be saved by Your Own blood, since You are also their cousin."

THE SONS OF SHEM

After the waters had drained away
enough, Shem took his father Noah
southward with him into the Middle East.
The journey took months, from Mount
Ararat to Hebron, though there were no
towns anywhere in the world at that time,
since every thing that had not been saved
within the Ark had been drowned, and
washed down into the ocean floor as the
giant temporary rivers drained all the
continents of the flood waters. Though
Shem was in his early sixties, Noah was
around one hundred and forty, and the
century of Ark-building had exhausted
him. The last of his tremendous strength
had been used very well to shepherd his
family and all the animals into the Ark
before the flood, and rule and sustain
them all while adrift for fourteen months
on the worldwide ocean, and after
landfall, to organize the evacuation of the

animals from the Ark, helping them all to find safe pathways down the steep sides of Ararat. For the first fourteen years, the animals still would not attack or eat each other, or any of the humans, but all lived for a while upon the huge store of grains that Noah and his sons had loaded into the Ark before the flood.

The final part of their adventure came to rest in what would later be called Mount Hebron. Noah lived another seven years there with Shem, before he fell asleep to take a nap in his tent one mild spring afternoon. When Shem came in later to wake his father for supper, the great old prophet was found quietly gone to be with the Lord. They buried Noah inside the mountain, and sealed the cave they used for his tomb with a deliberate landslide, so it could never be disturbed.

After a month of mourning, Shem took his two eldest sons, Elam and Asshur, and headed east to explore more of his new realm, leaving behind his five youngest sons and their sisters at Hebron, which had now become their home base. It took them over a year, but they went as far east as India, and then turned north until the impassable rock barricade of the Himalayas stopped them. After a few more months of exploration, astonished by all the spectacular scenery they continually found, they turned back westward to Hebron, longing for their other family members and home. As they journeyed, Shem watched his sons, now in their early thirties, discussing their dreams and plans for new kingdoms of their own, soon to be established at the locations of their choosing. The boys had always loved each other, and never had trouble between themselves, which was a great relief to Shem's heart, as he could never forget the trouble caused by his own brother Ham many years earlier. That foolishness had driven a wedge between the brothers, with Shem and

Japheth siding with their father Noah,
and Ham being driven away in disgrace.

Asshur was the younger of the two,
and far the wilder, always eager to try
some new daring thing, but not always as
dependable or responsible as Elam. Elam
had chosen to settle in the region south of
where Babylon would later be built, and
the region eventually was called Uz.
Asshur decided to wander far to the west,
and north, and within two years, he and
all his group reached a seashore in the
extreme northwest, and they could see
white cliffs across the channel of water
before them, so they built many small
ships, and ferried everyone over to what
would later be called England. Once
there, he found an open plain he liked,
and began to design and construct his
palace. The great foundation was built
with monster sized stones, and set in a
pattern of alignment that would prove
useful as a seasonal calendar, as the
patterns of shadows from sun and moon

slowly changed throughout the year. A large circular dike was built around the main structure, with a deep channel leading out from the front gate. The channel tied into a small river downstream, a few miles away, to provide a path for seagoing ships to approach the palace. The palace itself was made of wood, and rested high in the air upon the great foundation stones. Once the palace had been finished, a project that lasted twenty years, the entire area below it was flooded with the water that came pouring in, once they broke through the last bit of land between the channel and the small river. Now ships, if not too huge, could sail or be pulled like barges all the way from the sea right up to the base of the wooden palace, to load and unload cargo and people. That is, if Asshur and his growing army granted passage. Otherwise, the invaders could be easily pinned down and shot with arrows, since the ships could only turn around in the palace moat, which was more of a small artificial lake. The remains of the palace would later be called Stonehenge, and would confuse and mystify millions of people who would walk around the surviving foundation stones and fabricate all kinds of absurd theories about how and why the stones had been so arranged, and who could have possibly done it. No one guessed it was one of Noah's grandsons who did it within a century after the flood.

Meanwhile, Elam was busy in the land of Uz, building a great city, establishing trade, expanding his growing population, since food was very plentiful, and for many, many years, there were no serious outside threats to his kingdom. There was a crazy distant cousin of his to the north, named Nimrod, a legendary hunter, and fierce warrior, who was a giant, and an abomination. Nimrod was totally insane, and began to force all of his people to labor endlessly at the vain construction of a useless tower of bricks, attempting to reach all the way to Heaven itself. Nimrod worshiped the stars, the evil ones, and defied Almighty God in his madness. He called his large city Bab-el. Only once had he ever dared to assault Elam, but the Lord was with Elam, and Nimrod was wounded badly in hand to hand combat with Elam, while Elam's army killed around two thirds of Nimrod's army. Nimrod and his survivors retreated back to the north, and had just enough sanity to refrain from attacking Elam ever again. The land of Uz and the capital of Ur continued to grow and prosper, until it was the mightiest kingdom in the world, and dwelt in peace, since no one would dare to trouble it.

Years passed, and as Uz grew greater, Bab-el and Nimrod continued in their madness, always pushing the brick tower upward toward the stars. They invented a system of worship called astrology, which included forced human sacrifices and all kinds of abominable rituals of demon-worship. One night, after one such ritual, the demons within Nimrod told him to go attack Ur again. God was watching, and listening, and immediately smashed the tower to the ground, and the fallen bricks covered an area of over forty square miles. Those not killed in the disaster scattered in all directions, and somehow they could no longer understand each others' words, but they all seemed to be making just random senseless noises instead of sentences with meaning.

The centuries passed, and God was watching Ur, and the Chaldeans, until a many-generations-later descendant of Elam inherited the throne. This man loved God with all of his heart, and sacrificed unto Him daily, not only livestock and such, but also surrendered every wicked thought or emotion before the Throne of God. His people lived in blessing, and the man, named Job, became, in a few years, the greatest king in all the earth. Thousands of years later, people would call Job by the name Gilgamesh.

Then one day, the good Lord allowed the devil to send tornados to destroy Job's family and home, and Job lost everything, except his own life, and that of his wife. She was no help at all, though, and instead of comforting him, made his loss and misery much worse. Three of Job's closest friends, men whom he had trusted, decided to blame Job's catastrophe on Job himself, and spent a lot of the next year of his horribly ruined life finding fault with him in their so-called religious hypocrisy, all thinking themselves as pure from sin, but, as with Mrs. Job, being extraordinarily cruel to their broken king, even though all of them had previously profited from the high positions of wealth and power he had generously given them. Job was utterly alone in his unbearable pain, and it seemed like even his best friend, God, would not answer him any longer. This caused Job to search himself, to try to understand what he had done to deserve all of this horror.

Finally, one day when Job was alone, God spoke to him again, reminding him, by means of a pop quiz on the mysteries of Creation; that God was God, and Job was not. Job, a very intelligent and honest man, immediately humbled himself utterly before the Highest, and apologized for even daring to think of demanding explanations from God about what He was doing. God forgave his attitude, that he had thought God owed him answers, and once corrected in thought and word, healed his wounds and restored him, as soon as Job prayed for forgiveness to also be granted unto his so-called friends, and his wife, too. Over the next few years, Job was restored fully and much more, until he had twice as much blessing as he had originally. It is unknown whether or not he found a second wife.

The centuries passed, and the more recent Chaldeans became infested over time with the perversion of astrology, and the rulers tried to predict the future with the evil stars, as the Bab-elites had once done. God found a man, a true line descendant of Job, who with his son and all his family loved the true God of Heaven, and obeyed Him, keeping out of the witchcraft that was being practiced in their nation, which they now named Zoro-astrian, instead of astrology. Terah and Abram left the city of Ur behind, and following God's orders moved west to the city of Haran. They were prepared to go further, but Terah passed away in Haran, so God ordered Abram and his wife Sarah to bury Terah there, and continue westward. Abram and Sarah obediently did so, finally arriving at Mount Hebron, where Shem had made his city, and where Noah was buried in the mountain. The remainder of Abram's adventures can be found in Genesis. Through him came the Savior, about two thousand years later.

LAND OF GENERATIONS

After Terah passed away in Haran, Abram buried his dad respectfully, then obeyed the Lord and left his remaining family all there in Haran, except his wife Sarah, and his nephew, Lot. He moved toward the region of Shechem, until the Lord led him all the way to Alon Moreh, the mountain that would later be called Mt. Moriah. There He promised Abram that He would give him all the land to the north, all the way through and including Turkey, and the Black Sea, and all the land to the south, including all of the Arabian Peninsula, and the whole Sinai Peninsula, all the way to the Nile River, including the whole Red Sea, the Persian Gulf, and all the Mediterranean from Istanbul to the Nile. To the east the land would also stretch to the mountains of Persia. He also promised him that He would make Abram's descendants more numerous than the stars, and of greater number than the grains of dust upon Earth.

The land was the same region granted to Shem by his father Noah, after the flood waters drained away. Abram was a direct line descendant from Shem. God selected him to be the inheritor of all of Shem's territory, and the founder of the People of the Book, Israel. Abram believed God, and trusted Him to keep His Word, even when it looked impossible, and God gave Abram credit for righteousness, since he believed what God told him. As a sign of his new life of faith in God, God changed Abram's name to Abraham, which means "father of many nations" and showed God's future plans for Abraham.

Abraham built an altar there, and worshipped God, who had shown such loving favor unto him.

Two thousand years later, the Promised One would arrive, a direct line descendant of Abraham. He was born to be the final and eternal King of Israel. He is the final inheritor of all of Shem's territory. He was rejected by the religious hypocrites of His time, and because they were envious of Him, they framed Him, with lies, and had Him murdered.

Three days later He got up from His own tomb, spoke to all of His main followers several times, and ascended back to Heaven, where He was originally, before coming to earth.

He promised to return when the Day was precisely right, and things seem more and more to indicate that time could be fast approaching.

Whenever He arrives, He will rule from the same Mt. Moriah. About a thousand years after that, the City of Heaven, New Jerusalem, will descend and be placed permanently upon the earth. It will occupy forever the same family inherited lands that were specifically described unto Abraham. The center of the King's City will always remain Mt. Moriah, and the Holy Temple of the King of Kings. God's Word cannot be broken. As He has promised, so He will do.

THE PRODIGAL

He had been walking for several weeks. He was extremely tired, and if he were not a strong young man in his early prime, he would have stopped long before this landmark. As he topped the hill and saw it, his heart was renewed, and he knew he was almost home. Then doubts clouded his thoughts again, as he wondered exactly what sort of welcome he would receive, if any.

His brother had been furious when he left, but his dad had been quiet and sad. Oh, he had been given precisely what he asked, approximately half of the total wealth his father had built up over many years of diligent hard work and careful planning. The stress and aggravation between himself and his minutes-only older twin brother had finally reached a boiling point and exploded, over a local girl they both liked. In his opinion, it was smarter to just leave, go far away, and start a whole new life for himself. He was not sure if he would ever return, so he asked for his half of the inheritance, which would be plenty to fund a new start anywhere he wanted.

Things went okay for a while, but he drank too much, played around with too many expensive women, and, in a few years, his inheritance was gone. There were no telephones in those days, not even any postal services, either, so calling back home for help was impossible. Besides, the embarrassment his older twin would heap upon him was not something he wanted.

He had to hire himself to a rich Hittite citizen, to sleep out with the animals, and since he was a foreigner, he was made to watch over the pig herd. It was an abomination, according to his beliefs, for him to actually eat the pigs, so his boss figured he wouldn't steal any of them. The pay was a joke, the work was repulsive, and he barely had enough to buy food and clothing. Still, he stuck with it for more than a year, since no one else would hire him, and he had to eat. Then one night, as he accidentally fell asleep, after a very exhausting day moving the pigs from one area to another, for fresh feeding ground for them, disaster struck. He woke suddenly to the sound of squealing pigs trying to escape the desert cats that had followed the scent down from the nearby hills. Several pigs were killed, and some were dragged off by the family of big cats. The Hittite citizen was furious the next morning, and declared the young man would work without any pay at all, until he had covered the cost of the pigs lost. There were no labor unions in those days, either.

About four days later, weak from hunger, he asked his boss to share some food with him, and was denied. Like all the Hittites, the boss did not like Hebrews any, and they all remembered very well how he had lived the high life when he first arrived in Cappadocia. Now they were not going to miss the chance to kick him while he was down.

Two days later he had enough. He had survived all week long by foraging for food in the countryside, as he watched fearfully over the pigs, and had even thought of eating the rotting corn husks the owner gave the pigs he was fattening up for sale. He had to make his move, while he still had the strength to travel.

That night an hour after sundown, he took his little sling, a few good stones, the dagger he always wore, a walking staff, also good for combat, and headed back towards Hebron. He moved as swiftly as he could, determined to put as many miles between himself and the Hittites as possible before daylight. He hoped no more pigs would be killed that night, but his own life mattered more to him than swine. He knew very well that the Hittites would kill him for leaving the herd of pigs, if they could catch him. He also knew they would not willingly let him go, since he still owed them for several pigs.

Several hundred miles and a few weeks later, he began to enter the outskirts of his father's land, which was extensive. He had hunted small game along the way, having to move at night, and hide during the day, not certain of just how determined the Hittites might prove in their pursuit.

As he crested the last hilltop, and finally saw Hebron, his resolve strengthened, and he continued his epic march home. A few hundred yards from the town, he saw a figure running toward him, and at first felt a bit scared, thinking maybe his twin brother was running out to kill him. In a few more minutes he could discern enough detail to know it was instead his father, grayer and slightly heavier, but still strong and active enough to run to greet his son.

And then they were together! The boy began with lowered shameful gaze to say that he had sinned against heaven and done his father wrong, but the dad replied, "Jacob, my son, I forgive you! I thought you might be dead!"

They walked back to the house together, and Isaac commanded them to bring out the best robe, and put the family ring upon Jacob's finger, and kill the fatted calf, so they could cook the barbeque, to celebrate the return of the one they had thought was lost. As his many men followed his orders, Isaac spoke with Jacob of all his adventures and disasters, and the people with musical talent got out their instruments and began to play wild Hebrew celebration songs.

Esau heard the commotion way out in the field, and left the cattle herds in care of one of his father's men as he headed back to the house to find out what happened. Near the house, he grabbed one of the servants as he trotted past with some food items, and asked what made all the noise. When told that his twin brother Jacob was home again, safe and sound, and that his father Isaac had declared a holiday and a feast of celebration, he was enraged. He went back to the herd to sulk, determined not to celebrate his twin's return.

A little later, Isaac came out to speak with him, and finally calmed Esau down, by reminding him that he was always part of the family, and always had everything of his father's available to use as he saw fit. But he also corrected his hardened heart by pointing out that they had thought Jacob gone forever, and this miracle of his sudden return home was indeed just cause for great joy and celebration. Then they walked together back to the house to join the festival.

SMOKE

Then the LORD said to Moses, "Stretch out your hand toward heaven, that there may be darkness over the land of Egypt, darkness which may even be felt." So Moses stretched out his hand toward heaven, and there was thick darkness in all the land of Egypt three days. They did not see one another; nor did anyone rise from his place for three days.

Exodus 10: 21-23

As the battle raged between Moses and Pharaoh in the city of Memphis, about a thousand miles to the northwest, a Greek island named Thera suddenly began to quake violently. The shaking stopped, for about a minute, then the entire island exploded with the power of about

500,000 hydrogen bombs. A solid blast of super-compressed air raced outward in all directions, like a steel wall moving at hundreds of miles per hour. Everything within fifty miles died in seconds, either crushed and broken by the shockwave, or flash-baked in the 1800-degree pyroclastic gas that followed the shockwave. Most of the force of the blast went upward into the stratosphere, or southward. By the time the shockwave had existed for 20 minutes, it had weakened dramatically as it spread further out. When it slammed into the northern coast of Crete, it was only strong enough to break all the masts off the Minoan navy ships, and flatten any buildings not built of stone. Even some of the stone things still were broken and knocked down. Most of the Minoans on the north side of Crete were killed or seriously injured. The survivors did not have long to suffer, though, because within another half hour, the tidal wave from Thera scraped the entire island clear of anything that was not made of tons of stone, cresting over forty feet above the shore. There were few, if any, mourners for the dead Minoans, since they were well known all over the Mediterranean for their cruelty, and cannibalism.

The first mushroom cloud in human history still raced upward into orbit, but much of the smoke was driven to the southeast by the strong jet stream. Within two hours, it began to grow dark, very rapidly, all over Egypt. It seemed more like someone had drawn a huge curtain closed, shutting off the light, rather than a normal sundown. Everyone became terrified, and ran home into their houses, quivering in fear.

Since the sun did not rise the next day, the temperature continued to drop. At the end of the first 24 hours, the air was quite cool, about 30 degrees less than the day before. The dark was so thick that no one could see a person standing next to them.

There was the odor of burning rocks in the breeze. The Egyptians stayed in their beds, trembling, certain they were all about to die. After 72 hours, the temperature had dropped to twenty degrees and sleet was beginning to fall from the dark sky.

The insane tyrant still would not budge, until the Lord Himself came down unseen and personally killed all the first-born of the whole nation of Egypt, man and beast alike. Finally Pharaoh cracked, and commanded Moses to depart forever, and to also take with him every part and person of Israel, and never to return again. To this day, the children of Israel still celebrate the day the Lord delivered them from the hand of Pharaoh, and broke the chains of their captivity.

THE CHRISTMAS STAR

One night in the past, God said, "Gabriel, the time has arrived. Make haste, and go to the Earth, and announce the birth of My Son. Tell the chosen mother, Mary, first, then, after I have conceived Him, appear in a dream to His daddy, Joseph, and reassure him to hang on and stick with Mary through all things. Then go and appear as an exceedingly bright star to the wise men in the east, and lead them to Bethlehem, so they, who are also scattered children of Abraham, will follow and worship the Child. Also, appear with the whole honor guard unto the shepherds in the fields, since they also are His distant cousins. We will see to it that all His far scattered and long forgotten relatives are informed, so they can rejoice with Joseph and Mary that night."

Gabriel bowed his mighty head, and said, "Even so, Lord, for so it seems good in Your sight!" And immediately, he departed.

Less than a second later, Gabriel appeared to Mary, and announced the glad news to her. Less than a second after he was done speaking with Mary, Gabriel appeared in the night sky to the west of what had been once known as Ur of the Chaldeans. This time he did not mask his glory, but shown forth will all the honor and goodness inherent within one of the mighty cherubs of God, and all the other stars in the western sky were dimmed to invisibility by his light.

The eldest son of the ruler of that region had just stepped outside for a moment or two of prayer, before he turned in for the night. When the new star blazed forth, his jaw opened in amazement, and he fell to his knees, wondering what he was seeing. After the star continued to shine steadily for several minutes, the youth ran and woke his father, and made him come see, also.

After the initial shock wore off, the father said, "At last, the time is here! The God of Heaven has kept His ancient promise, and sent us His Holy Son, to save us! Wake up the royal guard, and have the servants and horsekeepers prepare right now! We are going to follow that star!"

The young man did as he was told, and the whole expedition, including the father and both his boys, as well as over 200 other men on horseback, departed within the hour, heading westward, following the great star. As daylight began to increase the star continued to shine clearly, easily visible even in daylight. The expedition kept moving until almost noon, when the ruler called the small army to a halt, and commanded the horses to be tended, and the men to also rest. They slept through the afternoon, and arose to make supper and eat. An hour later, they saddled the horses, mounted and resumed their westward march, still following the undiminished glow of the star, so bright, that they could actually read from the light of it.

They kept at their march for months, battling and killing many armed robbers and petty warlords who tried to attack and destroy them, and not one of the ruler's army was killed, though they fought many adversaries. There were three other kingdoms through which they had to buy and negotiate safe passage, since the small band of 200 could not overcome an actual army of one of the neighboring kings. Since most of their pathway was through mountains and desert, they were fortunate to make the journey in late winter, or the desert heat would have proved too great for men and horses. As the season turned from winter to early spring, they began to enter the borders of Israel, and decided to go straight to the local ruler, Herod by name, thinking that he would know and tell them where they could find the Child. As they turned at the fork in the road toward Jerusalem, instead of Bethlehem, the star winked out suddenly, causing them great distress.

At that moment, Gabriel and the rest of the King of Heaven's honor guard went and appeared to the shepherds in the field, and notified them of the great news. The shepherds forgot all about their herds in the sudden excitement, and immediately headed for Bethlehem, but the Lord had one of the angels stay there to protect the animals from predators.

By this time, the foreign ruler was done talking with Herod, and, as they left the outskirts of Jerusalem on the south road, the star suddenly appeared again, as abruptly as it had vanished, and stood over the manger, where the entire 200 men followed. When they arrived, most of the group stayed on the outskirts of Bethlehem, while the ruler and his two teenage sons went to the manger. The ruler told Joseph why they were there, and Joseph led them in to meet the Child, Who was resting in His mother's arms. They did not want to wake Him, but He opened His sparkling eyes and looked right at them, and laughed a happy little laugh as only a newborn could. Then He smiled at them, and continued to stare at them for several minutes, while the visitors fell to their knees, raised their hands to heaven, and began to sing an ancient hymn of thanksgiving in the Hebrew tongue. Joseph and Mary joined in the hymn, which was the Hallel, and it was one which they had sung all their lives, and the Child looked quietly from face to face as they sang. When they finished, He sighed contentedly, closed His eyes, and fell back asleep in Mary's arms. Joseph and the wise men quietly moved outside, so as not to wake Him again. The men gave many great and valuable treasures to Joseph, and noticed the approach of three shepherds. The shepherds had a look on their faces of men who had seen a vision, but they noticed that the wise men wore the look of those who have seen a dream come true.

The ruler and his sons rejoined the rest of their group, and told them all they had seen. As the men made camp for the night, each man was left with more questions than answers, yet they all felt a strange stirring deep inside, as though witnesses to the greatest moment in history, which indeed they were. During the night, Gabriel appeared to the ruler and his sons in a dream, telling them to avoid Herod at all costs.

The next morning, very early, the wise men and their army departed quietly toward home, and the town of Bethlehem, at least most of the people who dwelt there, never even knew they had been around, or what great thing had happened in the hours of the night.

LITTLE SISTER

She was married now. He was a really fine young man from a well respected family, even though they were not very wealthy. They were both in their middle teens, but that was quite normal in their culture.

Her whole family was there, except her daddy, who had passed away suddenly a couple of years earlier. Her oldest brother had filled in the best anyone could ever wish, as the leader and provider for the family, but she still missed her daddy, and she knew her younger sister did, too. They had a large family, full of love, with five brothers, and the two youngest were the sisters. Her oldest brother had just turned thirty a couple of months before.

Suddenly she noticed a man, one of the serving crew for the wedding feast, who approached her mother, and spoke quietly to her. Her mother's face became serious, then she hid it with a smile, nodded to the server, and went over to speak quietly with her big brother. He listened, made a quiet reply to their mother, smiled and got up from the table, and began to walk back toward the kitchen. Their mother motioned urgently to the servers, and ordered, "Do whatever He tells you!" while pointing to her son. They obediently followed Him into the kitchen.

A few minutes later, the servers came back, all carrying full pitchers of wine, with which they first went to the caterer of the feast, and had him taste it. After a sip, a smile of delight broke his intense expression, and he loudly proclaimed, "Most hosts will serve the good wine first, then after everyone has had a few cups, they serve the inferior stock. But you have kept the best wine until now!"

Her mother came up to her big brother, tears of joy in her happy eyes, and hugged Him. She said, "You just made them rich! What a wedding gift! Almost two hundred gallons of the finest wine anyone ever tasted! It's worth a fortune! They are set for life!"

He turned and smiled at His little sister and her new husband. All eleven of His closest buddies were staring at Him, stunned, speechless, as they realized what He had just done.

DEBT OF HONOR

There had been a time long ago when her family had been rich and influential, and well known all over the region. That had been a couple of centuries earlier, and things had changed. She was the last one of her family line, except for her son, a teenager who had been spending most of his last two years with his dad, who was her first husband. The couple had started out very young and in love, as teenagers at the time themselves, but had grown sadly apart as time passed. She had tried four more husbands after that, but never felt any lasting contentment.

As she walked down to the well with her water jar, she mused upon the stories she had heard as a child, about her distant ancestors, and, in particular, about one very rich merchant, who had later become governor of their region of Samaria. She remembered the tale about how he had once, in his youth, helped a wounded Hebrew man who had been left on the road to die by some cruel robbers. As he had bid farewell to the man, leaving him in the care of a local innkeeper, who was also a country doctor, the man had said, "You will be repaid in full." The merchant had smiled, and said, "We can settle up another day. For now, rest, and recover."

The well was not usually very crowded at midday, because the town was mostly home eating lunch with their families. Since she only had her boyfriend around these days, and he ate his sack lunch out in the fields where he worked, this was a good time slot to refill the water jar without waiting in line.

As she came around the corner of the well house, she saw a man she had never seen before, sitting there on the small bench, leaning against the well house wall in the shade. Their eyes met, and a quiet, friendly smile lit his face. He said, "Give me a drink of water."

She was stunned! The man was some sort of Hebrew rabbi or something, she guessed, judging by his clothing and accent. They never spoke directly to the Samaritans, because the Hebrews regarded the Samaritans as impure, since they had started out once as also Hebrew, but had, over the years, intermarried with the soldiers of occupying armies from Assyria or Babylon.

"Why are you talking to me?" she asked him.

"If you knew who was asking, you would ask me, and I would give you living water. Whoever drinks of this well's water will later be thirsty again, but whoever drinks of the water I give will never thirst again."

She replied, "Mister, I wish you really could give me that water, so I would not thirst again, nor have to keep returning to refill this jar."

He smiled a second, and said, "Go, call your husband."

Two minutes later, He smiled again, as He watched the woman run as fast as she could back toward the center of town, forgetting the jar that she was tired of carrying. Life for life, and mercy for mercy, the debt of honor was finally repaid. Israel's well was where the Spring of Living Water began to save Samaria. As it happened, the Hebrew man from centuries before had been one of His own distant ancestors.

LOAVES AND FISHES

The enormous crowd had listened eagerly. They wanted to hear and understand everything this strange, healing prophet had to tell them. His words helped them see and understand many things they had never even considered before. They had also seen Him work many unusual miracles of all sorts, and without exception, no person could lay a finger on Him, unless He permitted it. His words were so overflowing with wisdom and power, no one could listen to Him for more than a sentence or two without being irresistibly held captive, hungry to hear Him keep on speaking.

He noticed the people shifting restlessly, and sensed their growing fatigue, and hunger. He told His followers to make the people sit down in groups of fifties, and there were about a hundred of those groups. He told His followers to feed the people, and they replied that there were only five loaves, and two fishes, and what good could so little ever accomplish? Then He took the loaves and blessed and broke them, after looking up to Heaven and giving thanks to His Father. He gave the fragments to His followers, and they passed them out to the crowd, without ever running out at all. After that, He took the two fishes, and also gave thanks, then broke them into pieces to distribute to the followers, who gave it out to all the people, again without running out.

After they all ate until they were full, the Lord told His followers to gather up every fragment, so that none of God's blessing was lost, even as not one of God's children will be lost. When all leftovers had been gathered up, they filled twelve full baskets exactly.

The five thousand people are like the five thousand years, from Job, through

Abraham, Isaac, and Israel, all the way down through the centuries until the return of the King of Israel, and the beginning of His earthly reign. The five loaves are like the five Books of the Law, and the two fishes are like the two arrivals of the Son of God upon the earth. The twelve full baskets of the leftovers are like the redeemed of the Lord, which will help to fill up the twelve tribes of Israel, after all have been gathered up.

There was also another occasion where He fed another large crowd. This time it was four thousand people, and He started with a few loaves, and a few small fishes. When done, this time the leftovers were seven large baskets full.

The four thousand people were like the four thousand years from Abraham, until the coronation ceremony of the King of Kings in Jerusalem, on Mt. Moriah. The few loaves were like the books of the New Testament, and the few small fishes were like the apostles. The seven large baskets full of the remnant is like the seven-fold Spirit of God, giving the Gifts of the Spirit, and bearing the Fruits of the Spirit in our lives.

The Lord seemed surprised that the apostles did not manage to grasp the numeric symbolism of the totals involved in each case. To be fair, they did not, at that time, have the Holy Spirit to open their understanding of the things of God. That part happened later, after He was resurrected from the dead.

SEAMLESS

The day after the Sabbath, Lazarus gave Him a large supper to honor Him. Jerusalem was over flowing with people who had come from all over the Mediterranean, some of whom had traveled for weeks to be in town for Passover.

The next day, Monday, they all rose early, with much to tend for the coming holy week. He went up on the roof to pray as He watched the sunrise. As He thought about the coming spectacular days just ahead, which were planned and set before the world's foundation, He clearly heard His Father's voice in His thoughts. "Okay, Son, it's time. Have them bring Your war steed to You, and put on Your battle armor."

He immediately went downstairs, and told some of His followers to go and find the specific little gray donkey who had been chosen before the beginning of time, with exact directions as to where they would find him. As they left to do that, He went into a back room to change clothes. He took, out of a pack, the robe which His mother had woven for Him, made of one piece, from the top throughout, without seam. It had been blessed from the first thread prepared for it, and had been made according to the strict requirements listed in Leviticus. It was the robe of the High Priest, not of the order of Aaron, but of the Eternal order of Melchizedek, the king of Salem. He had to be properly attired when He rode into Jerusalem to intercede for the horrid sins of mankind.

As He finished dressing, His followers returned with the little gray donkey, and they took off some of their own robes and draped them over the donkey's back to make a rudimentary saddle for Him to use. He smiled at them, kicked off His sandals, then said, "Come on!" and mounted the colt. He turned toward the city's eastern gate, to ride through it and storm the enemy's stronghold, barefooted and single handed. He smiled as He rode. He knew that He would win. It would never be possible for death to hold Him.

THE FIG TREE

⁶He spake also this parable; "A certain *man* had a fig tree planted in his vineyard; and he came and sought fruit thereon, and found none. ⁷Then said he unto the dresser of his vineyard, 'Behold, these three years I come seeking fruit on this fig tree, and find none: cut it down; why cumbereth it the ground?' And he answering said unto him, 'Lord, let it alone this year also, till I shall dig about it, and dung *it:* and if it bears fruit, *well:* and if not, *then* after that thou shalt cut it down.'"

Luke 13:6-9

It was a bright, clear spring morning, with still a refreshing chill in the early air. He and His followers were walking up to the eastern gate of Jerusalem again, like, yet so unlike yesterday morning. Then He had ridden His young donkey colt into this same gate, but with a huge crowd of shouting and singing people lining the road, paving the way with tree branches and even some articles of their clothing. One day later, and especially very early in the morning like this, only a few folks noticed His quieter entry. A short distance before the gate, a little off to the side, there was a fig tree, which seemed quite full-bodied and healthy. He decided to grab a few fresh figs to munch as they finished their walk to the temple. When He arrived at the tree and looked up into it, He could find no figs fit to eat at all. The few that were even there were scrawny and dried out in appearance, or rotten and waiting to fall off the tree.

With great calm and dignity, He spoke to the fig tree, and said, "Let no man eat fruit of you hereafter, forever."

He then turned away, and resumed His march into Jerusalem. He went into the temple, and after a glance at the moneychangers and animal sellers, He quietly tied a few strong cords together at one end, and grabbed the knotted end, wielding the thing better than a cat-o-nine such as the soldiers liked. He turned all of their little tables over, and scattered all the animals from their places. He ordered them to get that crud out of His temple. The chief priests heard all the noise, and came running, demanding just who He thought He was, after all, to come in there tearing up their profitable little sacrifice-for-sale scam, so conveniently located right out there on the main porch. He told them He would prove He had the right to do all of those things, by raising Himself from the dead the third day after they killed Him, but they did not understand Him, or else they did not believe Him. Early in the morning of the first day of the next week, he would do precisely what He foretold, but the chief priests would still not believe Him, no matter what.

If the religious structure of Israel under the law was like the fig tree, He had also found useless fruit there. It was poorly formed, dried and shriveled, not nourishing or refreshing in any way, and was a disgrace to the tree which supported it. The same curse would apply to both trees, for the same reason.

From this time forward, the nourishing fruit would have to come from the True Vine, and all of its' many branches. The fig tree would remain withered, until a far future time when the Vine and the fig tree would be grafted together, and both could bear fruit in harmony.

That was enough for today. He would be back in the morning, with plenty more to say. All day tomorrow He planned to speak to the crowds in the temple porch, since that was Wednesday, and He already had unbreakable plans for a very special dinner, in an upper room, Thursday evening.

As He and His followers walked back out of the eastern gate, to go the short distance to Bethany, where they were staying as the guests of Lazarus, the disciples noticed in the late afternoon light that the fig tree just off to the roadside was completely dry and withered, as though it had not seen rain for a hundred years. One of the younger fellows ran over and grabbed a branch of it, and it crumbled to dust in his hand. They wanted to know, "How did it wither away so soon?"

He answered them, "Whatsoever you say, and do not doubt in your heart that it will come to pass, it shall be done."

CONNECTIONS

There was a very good reason that the servant girl at the gate had not stopped him. She wouldn't dare, not if she wanted to keep her good-paying job. She liked feeling important, and no one else wanted to watch the gate, not since they brought in the prisoner a few minutes ago. So she had taken it upon herself to go answer when someone knocked. As soon as she opened the gate, she saw the face of the young man standing outside. She had bowed her head respectfully. Then immediately, and silently, she moved back to let him walk into the courtyard.

He was no stranger here. Even though she was new here, and a very low-status employee in the household staff, every one of them had to know all the family members on sight. All of Israel knew old Annas, and his son-in-law Caiaphas, but those who worked here had to also know the two daughters of the High Priest. The older daughter had married a Pharisee solidly on the religious professional career path, and they had no children. The younger daughter was noticeably more rebellious, at least for a good Jewish girl, and had defiantly married a hot tempered, hard working, honest fisherman. They had two boys, now both young men, who worked with their father on his ship. The younger boy, John, was here everyday, bringing fresh fish for his grandfather, Annas, and the rest of their family. So when he was the one who knocked at the gate, she knew enough to bow and stand clear for him.

A little bit later, another man knocked, but she did not know him, and would not open the gate for him. John noticed the event from across the courtyard, and walked over. He asked through the gate who, and a muffled voice answered "Peter" and said no more. John told the girl to open the gate. She did. As Peter entered, he and John spoke quietly as they walked back into the courtyard, and the girl noticed that the man's accent was strange for the city. Perhaps he was from out in the countryside.

Less than an hour later, the servant girl accused Peter of being a follower of the prisoner, for the second time. She was trying to make herself look clever, and score some brownie points with her bosses. As Peter began to swear that it was a lie, a rooster crowed. John whispered in her ear to SHUT UP, since Peter would not have the same immunity from punishment that he himself had as the grandson of Annas, and the nephew of Caiaphas. No one would dare to lay a hand on John, but it would have gone very much differently for Peter, if he had been found out.

The next afternoon, there was a small group of people at the foot of the cross. There was the mother of Jesus, and Mary Magdalene, and John. No one in all the land of Israel, not the priests, not the soldiers, not the centurion, not anyone would say a word to the nephew of the High Priest, even if they thought it was strange that he was there. Because he was brave enough to go stand there, the women who loved Jesus also had courage to go stand and watch. For some strange and wonderful reason, no one said anything insulting or hurtful to John or the women, though they said horrible things to Jesus Himself.

Suddenly John remembered an embarrassing scene from a few weeks ago, when his own mother had gone to the Lord Jesus, asking for a favor from Him. She had requested that her two sons be allowed to sit, one upon His right, and the other upon His left, when He came into His kingdom. He had corrected her inappropriate request, revealing that the requested honor was already reserved for them to whom the Father had already given it. Maybe she thought it was a way to really show up her older sister, and that High Priest husband of hers, and also her dad, who was at the very least sort of stuffy, and way too traditional.

John's thoughts snapped back to the horrible present, when he heard Jesus call his name once. As he looked into his Lord's eyes, Jesus said, "Behold your mother," and nodded toward His own mother. Jesus then looked at His mother, and said, "Woman, behold your son."

After it was finally over, John took the mother of Jesus back to stay with his family, and she spent the rest of her life with them. Zebedee had learned to accept it when his sons had left fishing to go follow Jesus, and had become a believer himself. It was just fine with him, if the mother of the Lord wanted to come live with them, instead of returning to Nazareth.

THE THIRD CROSS

He knew very well that they deserved it. At the time, in the heat of the moment, it had all seemed right. After all, that Roman officer and his friends had it coming, just because they were Romans. Even if it had been Barabbas and Judas who had actually done all the bloodshed, he still had done his guilty part by obtaining the weapons they had used to do it, and telling the other two where and when the ambush could be easily done. Their motive was not money: they were zealots, and the Roman and his friends were the particular ones repressing a region of Israel where they suspected a rebellion, so the rebels had killed them. They had all been caught within a week, and sentenced to die. Then, for whatever reason, they had released Barabbas, even though the guy had been the ringleader of the whole group!

Now he and Judas were on their crosses, and between them was a man they had seen a time or two speaking to large crowds, and knew he was supposed to be some sort of prophet. How could that be true, if they were able to nail him also to a cross? The high priest and others stood there mocking and joking, insulting the prophet. The prophet met their eyes, with a calm, steady stare, but the priests could not look him back in the eye. Even Judas, hanging on a cross beside them, began to mock the prophet, too.

After a while, when all the stupid, nasty comments stopped for a minute, the prophet looked up to heaven, and said, "Father, forgive them, they don't know what they're doing."

Suddenly it hit him like a ton of bricks. The Man next to him really was innocent, and had never done anything wrong at all, in His whole life. And yet, He had just prayed for God to forgive those who were even right now murdering Him! No one had ever shown so much composure and grace in such agony before, refusing even to hate His own murderers.

At once, he shouted, "Shut up, Judas! Don't you even fear God? We're getting exactly what we deserve, but this Man did nothing wrong!"

Then he turned to the Prophet, and said, "Remember me, Lord, when You come into Your kingdom."

The Prophet looked him in the eye, and said, "This day you will be with Me in Paradise!"

THE CENTURION

He looked out over the entire port of Caesarea, and saw every activity happening in the town below. He was on the roof of his very nice house, which came with his office, as chief centurion of the Italian regiment. They were headquartered in this port town, where all kinds of provisions and reinforcements could land easily from Rome. For the last fourteen years, he had fulfilled all the duties of his commission perfectly. Now, as today was his fortieth birthday, he was in a reflective mood, and the strange events he had witnessed in this odd land filled his thoughts.

Like many of his soldiers, he had found and married a local girl, though her father had fought nearly to the death to prevent it. She was beautiful, and very intelligent, and, even though she loved him dearly, she made it clear she would never abandon the faith of her people, and insisted all their children, three sons and two daughters, would be raised as Hebrews, though because he was their father, they also enjoyed the enormous advantage of being Roman citizens. He often listened from the next room when his wife read the ancient scriptures and prophecies of her people to their children. He had learned Hebrew as a matter of practicality, and the scriptures stirred things deep in his soul that he could not understand.

One day, many years earlier, when he was new to his position, he and several of his men were riding patrol along the northern shore of the Sea of Galilee, when he heard of a Prophet in nearby Capernaum. This was not the first he had heard of this Man, and rumor had it that the Man could work many wonderful miracles, including all sorts of healings. He decided to go find this Prophet, since his mind was filled with the plight of his wife's younger brother, whom he had hired as manager of his estate. The young man was a fine manager, and the centurion loved him as though he were his own younger brother. Three weeks before this, the young man had fallen from a tall tree, where he had climbed to look for some stray animals from the centurion's herds. His spine had broken, and he was immediately paralyzed. The once vital and active young man could now only lay in extreme pain, helpless in bed. The entire family had been crushed by this, but the centurion still had to go about his normal business, while his wife tried to care for and comfort her little brother as best she could.

After a day of searching, they found the Prophet, teaching the local people in Capernaum about the coming Kingdom of Heaven. He approached the Man, and suddenly he was certain in his heart that this Man was the One foretold in the ancient scriptures. He asked the Man to heal his servant, and when the Prophet agreed, he was suddenly aware of his own sinful past, and he blurted out that he was not worthy for the Prophet to come to his home. So he asked the Prophet to just speak the command for his servant to be restored, and somehow he hoped that would do it. After all, if this Man was the One foretold, then He was also King of all creation, and everything and everyone was under His direct authority. No disease or injury of any kind could stand against the King of Heaven.

The Prophet did not seem surprised, so much as delighted, to find such great faith in the centurion, and He made a big comment about it, highlighting the fact that He had found great faith, even in a Roman. He told the centurion to go home, and that he would find his young brother-in-law fully restored. The centurion thanked the Prophet sincerely, and returned home. He indeed found it just as foretold, and the joy of his family was cause for the biggest celebration they had had since the wedding. The restored young man danced nimbly to ancient Hebrew songs at the party.

The next time he saw the Prophet, He was struggling to carry His own cross up the steep hill to be executed. Beaten, bloodied, and exhausted, the Prophet spoke no more, but strained under the heavy load of the cross. He stumbled once, and slammed down hard on one of His knees. As He gasped for breath, the centurion ordered a stranger to the city to help carry the cross. No one dared to contradict the centurion. It was his month to serve as the execution supervisor, a job not even the hardest Roman liked.

Over the next six hours, he sat stone-faced, watching the condemned prisoners die. Inside, he was full of pain and confusion. How could this mighty Prophet, in Whom he knew resided such miraculous power and authority, be possibly subject to such torture and death?

Halfway through, about noon, the sky grew dark and threatening, with great lightning and thunders, as though Heaven were about to wage war upon the whole earth. Then, about the hour of prayer, three in the afternoon, the Prophet gave a great shout, "Paid in FULL!" and died. The whole earth shook violently, and people screamed and ran for shelter, as large boulders split open, and a roar as of a great lion as large as the sky was heard everywhere.

The centurion said, "Truly this was the Son of God!"

The centurion finished his memories, and came down into his house to pray. It was about three in the afternoon. As he prayed, suddenly he was aware of someone else in the room with him. He lifted his eyes, and saw an angel of God. The angel called him by name, and said, "Send men to Joppa, to the house of

Simon the tanner, and ask for Peter to come here to you. Get your whole family ready to welcome him, and hear what he tells you, and do as he says."

The angel vanished as quickly as he had arrived, and Cornelius went downstairs to send his most trusted soldiers, and his brother-in-law, to go find Peter.

SPRINKLED

It was the ultimate judo-type maneuver. By allowing the enemy to kill Him, all of His people would be safe. The King was the only one who could accomplish this impossible mission. No one else was clean from sin, not since the Eden disaster, and no one else in Heaven or earth was tough enough to take it without fighting back. He knew before it happened, and every second that it dragged on and on for hours, He was constantly aware that He could indeed stop it at any time, and have all His tormentors killed most horribly, just by saying the Word. His mission was not to kill them, but to forgive and save them. Some would later understand, and change, but most would not. He had come to give everyone a fair chance, but to pay for only the ones who would hear and obey His commands.

When He was praying in the Garden of Gethsemane, He had not felt fear, but extreme sorrow. There was still so much Life left to live down here, but it would have to be given up for a couple of thousand years, in order to allow the congregation to grow from eleven men to billions of people. It would suit Him fine once it was all finished, but it was not going to be much fun for the next few hours. The thought of the physical agony was depressing, of course, but the really loathsome part of it for Him was that His own Father was going to entirely abandon Him, for about fourteen hours, from about one in the morning until three in the afternoon, which is the hour of prayer. For Eternity, He had lived with His Father in righteousness, but now He was about to be smeared with stinky sin, the sin of all who would someday be saved, your sin and mine. That was the part that was so disgusting, that it made Him want to puke.

So, at about nine in the morning, on a very cold early spring day, they stripped Him completely naked, laid Him down on a wooden cross, and drove large spikes into His wrists and feet. When they drove the spike into His left arm, one drop of His blood splashed to the ground. When they drove the spike into His right arm, one more drop of His blood splashed to the ground. When they drove a spike through both of His feet, two more drops of His blood splashed to the ground. When they lifted up the cross with Him pinned to it, and slammed the bottom eighteen inches of the cross into the hole prepared for it, three more drops of His blood fell from His beaten and bloody head.

Once a year, on the Day of Atonement, the high priest went into the holy of holies, and sprinkled the mercy seat with seven drops of blood from the sacrifice.

When the seventh drop of His blood hit the Earth, the planet, for the very first time since Eden, was once again sanctified unto the Lord, and the purification process began immediately. It was so toxic and contaminated with millennia of sin, that it would take a couple of thousand years of hard work before it would even be marginally fit for Him to openly rule upon again.

When the hour of prayer arrived, three in the afternoon, the prayer He prayed was, "Father, forgive them, for they know not what they do."

Then He shouted, "Paid in FULL!!!" and died for us.

A few days later, just before the resurrected Son of God ascended to Heaven, He told His disciples, "All power and authority in Heaven AND EARTH is given unto Me!"

Remember, this is no longer enemy territory. Seven drops of the King's blood changed all of that, forever. Earth has been sprinkled.

THE WIDOW'S MITES

The old lady went into the temple to make her small offering. She had heard that the Lord was there today, and she hoped to thank Him for the healing he had given her a couple of years earlier. That day had changed her life in a split second. She had, in desperation, reached out and grabbed the hem of His robe, a lawful, priestly robe, woven without seam from the top throughout. In that split second of contact, power from the King of Kings had flowed like a lightning bolt into her body, and the years-long sickness deep inside her had vanished. She confessed her desperate act unto Him, when He asked, "Who touched Me?" He had smiled at her and told her to go in peace.

Two years later, she was still healed, and much more active and stronger now that she was not continually losing blood because of the disease. So she wanted to see Him again, and thank Him for His compassion and help. There were very many people there today, since it was the week of Passover, and she did not see Him for the moving crowd. She waited patiently in line, and when it was her turn, she placed all she had left in this world, only two small coins, known as mites, into the treasury. She was embarrassed that she had no more to give, but the years of the disease, and the outrageous fees the so-called doctors had charged her had left her completely broke. She and her husband had once been very well off, until his accidental death, and after that, her hellish disease. Still, she was so very thankful for being made well, she wanted to give everything she had.

Even though she did not see the Lord in the bustling crowd, He saw her. Also, He remarked that her offering was the greatest one given that day.

Later that same week, as Nicodemus, the Chief Scribe of Israel, and his friend Joseph of Arimathea, the Chief Treasurer of Israel, were moving the body of Jesus to the Tomb, the two members of the Sanhedrin talked about what things they needed, to complete the burial ceremony for the Lord Jesus. The unused tomb was the property of Joseph. Joseph mentioned that they had all the spices and even the royal burial shroud ready, since those things were kept always ready for the death of one of Israel's kings, but they needed a couple of small coins to place upon the Lord's eyes when they entombed His body. Joseph went into the treasury, and came back out with the two small coins that the widow had given a few days earlier. As they laid the body of Jesus upon the first half of the fourteen foot long shroud, Joseph and Nicodemus each placed one of the small coins upon the closed eyes of the Lord, so they would not open as rigor set. Then they closed and sealed the tomb with the small army of men they had brought with them, and the only offering left in the tomb with the Lord was the two widow's mites.

REACHING THE LOST

They arrived quickly at the entrance to the cave. He stopped and turned to speak to the two honor guards with Him. Most people who came here were dragged here screaming and terrified, helpless to escape the evil angels that carried them here after death. This Man had arrived with calm dignity, escorted quietly by two of the mighty cherubs, Gabriel, and Michael.

"Thank you, friends. Wait here while I go correct the lies of the enemy, and show all the captives the Truth. I will return in a couple of days."

The Man then turned and began to calmly walk down the long, black tunnel into the huge dark cave. As He walked, a very bright light began to glow from Him, and shined brighter until He was glowing from head to toe, and was brighter than the noonday sun. As the

light began to glow out from Him, His
footsteps began to shake the ground,
harder and harder, until even the walls of
the tunnel and the cave began to crack
apart. Millions of screams were heard
coming from the darkness, as the evil
spirits began to scurry to find rocks under
which to hide. All of them, and there
were many, were absolutely quaking with
panic. They knew precisely who this Man
was, and not even all of them together
were brave enough, or fools enough, to
try to attack Him directly. He stopped at
the entrance out of the tunnel into the
main part of the gigantic cave, and stood
still looking around at all the cowering
evil things, since His eyes were like red
lasers, and saw though everything upon
which He looked.

Suddenly, louder than all the deafening
cries from the demons, there came a
noise like a monster tornado, a
tremendous jet engine, and a roaring bear
all combined. From around a corner near

the far end of the cave, several miles away, there emerged a giant, flaming, screaming ugliness of a thing, so repulsive to see that it made the mind and heart want to vomit at first sight. The sight and the sound of the beast were so perversely wrong that no sane mind would ever want to encounter the thing. Of all the ugly, sub-human swine of the evil spirits, only the dragon of ugliness was not afraid of the King.

The King calmly stood His ground, as the stinking pervert of all time charged at Him, screaming blasphemies, and spraying a liquid stream of fire out before it as it ran. The King waited a few seconds, until the beast was about half way across the whole expanse of the cavern, and then He said, in a normal, calm tone of voice, "Sit down, and shut up." Even though He said it as though in a quiet conversation with a friend, everyone and everything heard Him clearly, and all the noise immediately stopped. In the sudden and solid silence, a dull thud was heard, as the big dragon fell out of the air to the rock floor of the cave, shaking the place upon impact. The fire from the animal's mouth was snuffed out instantly.

The King said to the dragon, "I told you once before. You are NOT the God of Fire. I AM!" When He said this, the entire place trembled violently, as though about to collapse and cover them all.

The dragon whimpered, then growled, then sprang up again to once more charge at the King, but without even any wisp of smoke or flicker of flame this time.

This time, the King leaped forward to meet the dragon halfway to Him, and with a classic John Wayne style fist smashed the dragon in the face, breaking its' nose and cheekbone. The huge worm screamed louder than ever before in its' long life, this time in pain, and terror. Like all the cherubs, this one had also been made without fear, but now it was afraid, for the first time in its' evil life. It knew for certain now that it was eventually going to die. It knew it actually could feel pain. It knew that Someone could beat it. Now it knew that this Man was that Someone, and that He was the One Who was going to kill it, someday, maybe even today.

The King walked calmly over to where the enormous worm was cringing in a ball on the floor of the cave, terrified of Him, and reaching down, He yanked the keychain off of the worm's armored belt. Holding the keys aloft in one hand, He reached down with the other, His left hand, and grabbed the dragon by the ankle. He then began to drag the worm up and down throughout the length and breadth of the great cavern, proclaiming, "Repent, for the Kingdom of Heaven is at hand!"

As He did this, all the other evil spirits remained silent and trembling, stunned by what the King had just done to their boss. There were others listening and watching, also. Among the other hapless creatures in the dungeon of hell were many human beings, some of whom had already been there for thousands of years. Their chains had all fallen off the moment the King had taken back the keys from the enemy. Now, with the demons held silent and motionless, the humans, suddenly freed from their chains, began to come and gather near the King, as He had found a small hill top within the cave and was beginning to preach the Gospel of the Kingdom of Heaven to all of them. He told them all about Himself, and His Holy mission to save people, and that when the time came, He would separate light from darkness, once and for all. He preached to them for two straight days and nights, and no one moved or interrupted Him. The demons kept their hands over their own ears, and their eyes shut tight, but they did not dare to interfere.

After two days of preaching, He told them it was time for Him to return, be resurrected, and fulfill all the prophecies. He promised that on the Day of Days, He would see into each heart, and know those who had loved Him, and had heard His words and obeyed Him, and that they were going to have Life, and not death, for Eternity. He told them that He would come back once, and only once, more, and next time, remain forever, ruling openly over Heaven and Earth. He told them not to give up, no matter how things looked, or felt, until He came back in glory with the good angels, after the sun and the moon both went dark. He also warned them not to allow themselves to be deceived by clever liars any more.

Then He told them all, while looking sternly at the devil, that He, and He alone had ALL authority in Heaven and on Earth, and the Earth, which was lost to evil in the time of Adam's kingdom, was now rightfully and lawfully reclaimed for mankind by the Son of Man, and was no more part of the devil's territory.

Then He turned, and for the first time in the history of Creation, became the only human, yet, to ever walk out of hell.

THE LITTLE BANG THEORY

The two research physicists were locked in intense discussion. Each one was sure he was correct, and trying vainly to persuade the other.

"What do you mean, a singularity?"

"You know, a point source, a collapsed space curve, a black hole, or something."

"Or something?"

"Well, something that curves space, just like that. An intense enough energy blast could theoretically produce the same effects as an intense mass concentration, but no one has ever observed anything like that, or even has any idea how such a tight bundle of energy could occur."

"So why do you even think there was a point source of any kind?"

"Tidal effects."

"What?"

"Because, we know for certain that the image on the Shroud is NOT paint, or any kind of chemical, but was a flash-searing of just the very outer ends of the fibers in the Shroud material, and, because the image is a perfect one-to-one, photo-negative, life-sized recording of the moment of Resurrection, and the image is photo-accurate, front and back, to the finest details. That could not possibly be so, unless the Shroud were stretched out flat, like two pieces of plywood, both above and below the body, at exactly the same moment, and the body itself were suspended in midair a few inches above the slab. The only places where tidal forces of such intensity are to be found is very near to black holes, which would be able to produce that much close-range tidal difference between top and bottom of structure. Therefore, at the center of the body mass, there must have been a momentary surge of energy in the structure of creation, so powerful that it momentarily changed the laws of energy, time, space, and matter, from even the rarest states, to something we have never seen before. The concentration of energy required to achieve that, in the estimated quadrillionth of a nanosecond that the flash lasted, is mathematically somewhere near the magnitude of the original Big Bang!"

"Preposterous!"

"Check the math yourself, if you want, but we've done it many times. The evidence does not lie."

"Why, then, were all the planets in the Solar System, including the Earth, not instantly incinerated?"

"Because of the incomprehensibly short duration of the flash, or any longer, and we all would have been hot plasma vapor, moving outward at light-speed."

"Wow."

"Yeah, wow! Think about this, too. Like the original Big Bang, that Little

Bang had to have produced a shockwave, radiating outward in all directions. It's been traveling outward for about 2,000 years, now. How are we to know that the bulk of the force from the shockwave is not traveling in perhaps another dimension, and effecting extreme changes in the unseen parts of Creation? Our instruments cannot measure what they cannot see."

"I want to check your math, but you do make a convincing case. So, what do we do about this shockwave? Get ready for the world to end?"

"Not so much end, as change. We do not know, and cannot even guess, exactly what changes, or how soon, or how much. But change will occur. We should pray that the changes are for the better, and that we ourselves change in the right directions. Nonetheless, change will occur. For thousands of years, no big changes happened in the world, but then, Jesus came back from forty days in the wilderness, and the first thing He commanded was, 'Change!' And the changes have never stopped happening since He said that. There is also another thing or two which He mentioned. He said, 'Behold, I make all things new!' Maybe this is one way in which He literally is reforming His Creation, at the sub-atomic level, from the inside out. He also said that He is the Alpha and the Omega. That means the beginning and the end. He started Creation, and He's surely going to see to it that it finishes up precisely the Way which He planned it all along!"

THE STRONGEST CHERUB

They are very large. When one of them stands upon the earth, his head is actually in space. In a single stride, they can walk from one continent to another. When they go forward, they walk through everything else that was created, without slowing down. They can fly through the heart of stars, and not be burned. They can walk upon the clouds without falling through, and they can somehow move from any point in the universe to the far side of the universe in the blink of an eye, as though space and time were as easy for them to walk through as the solid mountains upon the earth, which to them are as a thin cloud. Their eyes can see into the center of the earth, and can directly perceive entire clusters of galaxies at once, and also look down deep into the subatomic scale, and clearly see the quarks and mesons and bosons, and even focus clearly upon each individual electron racing at light speed around the nucleus of an atom. They are the very mightiest of all creatures, so strong that only two others of their own kind can stop them. Their heads are scary to behold, with the face of a man in front, though as though formed of solid lightning, and the face of a ram on one side, and the face of a lion on the other side, and the face of an eagle on the remaining side. Their bodies are covered from head to toe with eyes that see everything. When they move, faster than thought, they move like a rook on a chessboard, not turning, but traveling in a straight line through anything.

Only four of them were ever made, or ever will be. They are the cherubs of God, and they are not the cute little flying babies that people wrongly call cherubs.

They were created for specific purposes, mainly to attend to God and His royal throne continually. Not to take care of Him, (how ridiculous) but to hear and obey Him immediately, no matter what. They were all four made without any fear at all. They were the only things created that cannot ever feel fear, not even of God, or they could not stand in His presence without trembling.

The first one created was the Cherub of Energy, or Light. He was made when the Lord shouted, "LIGHT!" That moment was also later called the Big Bang by men. One trillionth of a second later, the Lord said, "TIME!" and the Cherub of Time was formed, as the Light began to expand. Then the Lord said, "Space!" as the expansion accelerated outward, and the Cherub of Space was formed. Finally, the Lord said, "Matter!" as the energy, time, and space began to condense into little packets of some solid material, and the Cherub of Matter was formed. As time passed, the Lord formed more creatures, millions of them, whom He called angels, though they were not nearly as mighty as the Cherubs. He named every one of these creatures, and knew every thing in their hearts and minds continually. They each one loved Him completely.

The Creator then declared, as a warning to all creation, "Let Us make man in Our Own Image!" as Father, Savior, and Holy Spirit began to shape man. Every creature was clearly warned to not interfere. The Lord made man through His Word, fabricated out of the energy, time, space, and matter which He had made already.

As space contracts, time slows almost to a stop. As space expands, time accelerates. The action of the energy focuses the direction things go, whether to expand or contract.
From the Throne of God, only six days passed. From man's viewpoint, racing outward in the expansion wave, fourteen billion years passed. How appropriate

that from Adam to the end, fourteen billion humans would live and die.

When Adam was made, He spoke face to face with God. When one of the cherubs was upon earth, Adam easily saw and spoke with them, also. Not only that, they had to obey Adam's orders when they were anywhere even close to earth, even within the solar system. That was why the enemy, one of the cherubs, the last one made, and the weakest of them all, could not assault Adam directly, but had to use deception to destroy him. Even then, it had to get to him through his beloved wife, who did not have the long experience and time alone with God that Adam had known for centuries before she had been created. Adam made the same mistake that many, many men have also made since then, and obeyed his wife, instead of God. We have been suffering the results of that disobedience ever since.

The enemy did it because of his pride, and because he envied Adam, and likely thought that the cherubs were not being honored enough, since God had made this upstart thing out of dirt, and even called him His son. The enemy knew no one, not even all creatures together could overthrow God, so he hatched a scheme to kill Adam instead, realizing that if he could make Adam disobey, he would have to be killed to fulfill justice. The very first shot fired in the War of Heaven and Earth was when the enemy came and tempted Eve. A third of the angels were persuaded that they wanted in on it, and quietly joined up with the enemy. God was silently watching all of this, though they did not perceive that they were being observed from the Throne.

God sent two of the cherubs, Gabriel, the Cherub of Time, and Michael, the Cherub of Space, to defeat the enemy and drive it from the Garden. God spoke, and the enemy was immediately changed from the Cherub of Matter to a much weaker thing, and it was ugly, and it stank with evil. Its' name was changed from Lucifer to Satan.

The two thirds of the angels which remained faithful also fought against the rebel angels, crushing them and driving them far out of the Garden. God came personally to Adam and told him what would then occur, as a direct result of their treason. Adam could no longer look God in the eye because of his shame.

The greatest of all the cherubs, Eden-el, was commanded to stand guard over the Garden, and, in particular, the Tree of Life. That cherub is so exceedingly strong that he can single-handedly destroy everyone else that might ever try to enter the Garden, even, if necessary, all the other cherubs, and everyone else, at the same time.

Eden-el can not be defeated by anyone but God Himself, though that cherub is absolutely loyal to the King of Kings, and there will never be any conflict between him and our Maker. The mightiest creature ever made is still on duty, never sleeping, never tired, since his power, authority, and strength stream continually from the Lord directly. He will never leave his post, or fail, and the Garden will remain secure until the time when the Son of God commands him to unlock it.

LENGTH, WIDTH, AND DEPTH

We know, from His Holy Word, that Almighty God is One, but manifests Himself to His creation as Father, Savior, and Holy Spirit. That is how Jesus commanded us to go and make disciples of all the nations, in the Name of the Father, the Son, and the Holy Spirit. In addition to that, we also have all His mighty works as Father, and all His mighty works as Son, and all His mighty works as Holy Spirit for additional proof.

There was an occasion when the hypocrites came to Jesus and tested Him, showing Him a coin after asking Him whether or not to pay taxes to Caesar. He told them that since the coin had Caesar's image and name on it, it belonged to him, so pay it to him. He also told them to render unto God that which is God's. Now what is it that has God's Image and

Name upon it? The answer, according to Genesis, is mankind.

Of course, you're likely thinking that we all do not seem to much resemble Almighty God, some perhaps less so than others. Not only are we so extraordinarily frail and weak, we are severely limited in all ways. We do not live very long, and we keep on making the wrong choices, sometimes stubbornly, even when we really know better. Even when we love, it seems at times to contain a selfish motive, or a hidden agenda. Obviously, these observations do not apply to any of you who are already perfect, Lord Jesus.

But for myself, and the rest of you folks, we just cannot seem to get it right, or, even if we do, we cannot maintain it for very long, before, like a baby, we lose balance, and fall flat on our butts again. Hopefully, over time, and with practice, we fall down less often, and less hurtfully. Babies want to walk, so they keep trying. We want to walk in faith, with wisdom, so we have to keep trying, too. The less time we spend sitting on our rear ends, crying about falling down, the sooner we can get up and start trying to walk again.

Anyway, back to the image concept: the creature known as man is composed of three essential components. Body, soul, and spirit are the ones listed by Jesus. He warned us to fear the One who, after He had killed, had Power to destroy both body and soul in hell. Of course He is referring to Himself in His future role as Judge at the Great White Throne. For the humans who have been ALLOWED, by the grace and free, we did NOT earn it, gift of God, to become born again, we have a spirit born of the Father. Notice Jesus did not say He would destroy human spirits in the fire, only bodies and souls. The soul is the combination of heart, mind, and personality, and is the individual identity of every living creature, not just mankind.

There are many other ways in which the Creator has stamped His "THREE" on parts of reality. Space has length, width, and depth. Time has past, present, and future. Normal matter has three states: solid, liquid, and gas. Earth presents land, sea, and sky. The basic solar system is the earth, the sun, and the moon. Human life is life, death, and afterlife. The primary projective components of light are blue, red, and green. The essential atomic structures are electron, proton, and neutron. The fundamental human family structure is a man, a woman, and children. The children only get one vote, since they don't help pay any bills. Even within the space dimensions, such as length, there are three subdivisions: forward, backward, here. Or, as in width, it might be described as right, left, middle. Elevation might be thought of as up, down, level. Perhaps you will notice more ways that our Maker has stamped

His "THREE" on things He made. These are just some that I noticed over the years. One strange application of this pattern is even seen in our living physical bodies. In order to remain alive, we must have respiration, circulation, and communication (nerves). To remain alive for a while, we must have ingestion, digestion, and elimination. In our daily life patterns, we must have nutrition, exercise, and rest.

The unavoidable conclusion of all that observation is this: everything; and I do mean EVERY THING, that does exist, actually does belong to Almighty God. So, every bite we ever ate, every sip we ever drank, and every other good thing we ever had or will have belongs to God, and it is only because He is very good, and very generous, that we ever had anything to enjoy at all. May I suggest that we thank and praise Him, for every time we have any good thing that we are given. Maybe, at the least, say a quiet silent thanks to Him. We owe it to Him, you know.

What about Jesus and you? Do you realize He even made and owns the atoms of your body? What is it that you have that He did not make for you? Nothing!

Remember not to withhold your obedience from Him. It is the one thing you can actually choose to give, or withhold, from Him. You believe only because He allowed you to do so. You did not choose to believe. You love Him because He first loved you. You did not choose Him, but He chose you. That's what He said. God does not make you choose to obey. He does not want robots. So, when you choose to obey His Words, you are giving Jesus the only thing that is really yours to give. You are giving Him respect, and you show it by hearing and obeying what He told us to do. Just as your obedience is yours to give, so is your disobedience. He told us which one He wants. I personally do not want to withhold anything from the One who made me and saved me, and gave me every good thing I ever had in my life.

Also, He said not to call Him Lord, but ignore what He commanded. If you love Him, you will obey Him. You cannot be saved by His Cross, if you will not bow before His Crown.

THE COLOR CODE OF GOD

Why is the sky blue? Why is grass green? Why does the green leave the grass when it dries out or dies? Why is the blood of every person in the world the exact same red color, no matter what color their hair, or eyes, or skin may happen to be? Why is it that we often see both blue and red in the sky, but never green, except in rare exceptions? Why can white light be separated into three discreet components, which are blue, red, and green? Why do I ask you to consider these things?

These are the kinds of questions a child might ask, but they are the things an adult might skip right past, without noticing. A scientist would want to tell you about how the green comes from chlorophyll, and the red comes from red blood cells, and the blue comes from dust particles in the air refracting and scattering the light. That would all be factually correct, but still does not answer why. Why were those particular colors assigned to those particular chemicals, dust particles, or whatever is showing the color?

We know that God is Light. When Jesus is described during the transfiguration, and again in Daniel, and again in Revelation, He is said to have hair and beard whiter than snow. We are told that God dwells in unapproachable light, where no man can enter. We are told that God wraps Himself in light as with a garment. We are told that His Eyes are an unbearable, hot fire. God reveals Himself as Three in One, and One in Three. One person, always the same, without ever changing, yet He is able to simultaneously become, and remain, Father, and Son, and Holy Spirit. He is the same person, yet shows Himself in our lives as Father, Savior, and Very Best Friend.

In His role as Father, He created Heaven and earth, and all that is in them. That is the real reason the sky is blue. That is why the ocean is blue. When we see the beautiful vastness of the sky and sea, we are constantly reminded of how great and enormous and beautiful our God indeed reveals Himself to be.

What about the red in our blood? That corresponds directly to the color code of the Son. We are told in the scripture that God has made all men everywhere of one blood, that through the blood of the one man, Jesus Christ, all men can be saved.

As far as the projective primaries go, that only leaves green unmatched. The Holy Spirit is color-keyed to green. Green is the color of the healthy, growing, fruit-bearing things down here on the surface of the earth. If you look at the NASA space survey photos of earth for each month of the year, you can see how the entire temperate regions of the earth change color with the seasons. It's like watching the planet live, then die; then live again.

Back to projective primaries: when blue, red, and green light beams of equal strength are combined and overlapped, the result is a pure white light. When one beams white light into a prism, then, out will come blue, red, and green.

Coherent light is when all the wavelengths of the emitted light are in perfect synchronization with each other. In our modern world, we call such a thing a laser. Mankind has never found a naturally occurring laser in the universe, yet. It seems quite possible that if we had instruments that could see and measure into the supernatural realm, beyond the three percent of the total light spectrum that our physical eyes can perceive, and even beyond the known physical electromagnetic spectrum, where some of our modern detectors can sort of see a little bit, perhaps we could actually witness some of the unseen glory of it all.

Who, but God alone, could even begin to imagine what frequency at which He oscillates, or even if He does oscillate, or not?

The deep black of outer space is now known to be not actually totally dark. Even in the coldest, darkest, furthest-out-there places, there is still a dull red glow of three degrees Kelvin above absolute zero. It is supposed to be the leftover afterglow from the initial Big Bang, when Father said "LIGHT!" We are told that Father made all things through Jesus, and there was not anything made that was not made through Him, and that He is the True Light from Whom all things are made. We are told that the Light still shines in the darkness, and the darkness cannot snuff Him out. The blue of the sky and the sea reminds us that Father made the whole creation, but the dull red glow in the entire universe reminds us that the whole thing was made through the Son.

Upon the surface of the earth, we see blue, red, and green, and the Creator works here among us as Father, Son, and Holy Spirit, but in the sky we do not usually see green.
What our earthly eyes can see in heaven is the blue of the Father, the red of the Son, and the gold of the glory of God. The green of the Holy Spirit is only seen upon the Earth, because that is the only place He is working.

THE SEVEN FACETS OF THE JEWEL OF TRUTH

At the very core of all reality, at the inmost center of that which indeed does exist, there is a very great Jewel of Light. The spectacular Stone does not reflect light, it is the Source of Light, and even though it transmits out blue, red, and green as intensely as giant lasers, the overall effect is a dazzling, pure white, with a brilliant golden glow of an aura all around it like a glowing sphere containing the Stone.

The Stone lives, and breathes, and moves, turning slowly in space. The tightly bound beams of light of which all solid matter is built had their origin in the Stone, and went out where they were sent by the Stone, and became what they were commanded to be. Neither did the faithful light beams change, but steadfastly remained in the orders of the Stone. One thing did later choose to go sour, and led a brief rebellion. It will soon be squashed, forever.

Because the Stone is beyond human perception, and by its very nature supernatural and deeply mysterious, the Jewel's existence is both in the physical realm, and much, much beyond it, also. It is also impossible for a normal human mind to perceive all of the facets of the Jewel at once. That is often one reason why one person may see an aspect of the Truth, and be convinced that there is no other possible viewpoint on the matter. Another equally convinced and sincere person from another perspective may also perceive one aspect of the Truth, a different aspect of the Truth, and also know that he knows that he is right. This can lead to terrible conflict, even among the most sincere of believers, and is where all the different denominations came from.

Why seven? Why seven lights on the true minora, as specified in the Old Testament? Why seven days in a week? Why seven Days of Creation? Why seven candlesticks in the vision in Revelation?

The answer is found in the list of the seven gifts of the spirit. The list of the Gifts of the Spirit is as follows: prophecy, healing, exhortation, teaching, giving, leadership, and showing mercy. In some translations, healing is called ministry, but the original word is healing.

During the first Day of Creation, the Maker created Light. The first of the Gifts of the Spirit is prophecy. Prophecy is light. The first thing God said is "Be there Light!" We know that was a command, since the light is still shining. It is also a prophecy, true in the sense there will always be light from then on through eternity, and it will never be extinguished, or burn out, or flicker or fade.

In the second Day of Creation, God made the firmament, and called it Heaven. The second of the Gifts of the Spirit is healing. Since one of the primary proofs of His true identity as God in the flesh was all the healing King Jesus did while He was preaching (exhorting) and teaching during His time here, we can certainly see the association between Heaven and healing. In the Word of God it says, "You are the Lord who heals us."

In the third Day of Creation, God made the seas gather together, and the dry land appear, and He made the green grass, herbs, and trees bearing fruit, each according to its kind, to spring forth, and bear fruit. The third of the Gifts of the Spirit is exhortation, one of the primary purposes of preaching. Encouraging ourselves and others among the family of Jesus to deliberately choose to bear good fruit for the honor of Him Who saved us is one of our main responsibilities.

Notice how the Father is the One Who sends and completes the prophecy, the Son is the One Who brings, gives, and is healing, and the Holy Spirit is the One Who encourages us to bear fruit of good works based on faith, and motivated by gratitude. The Holy Spirit also enables us to do the thing we need to do, especially if we can never do it on our own.

In the fourth Day of Creation, the Maker made the greater light to rule the day, and the lesser light to rule the night, and all the stars of heaven, and He set them for times, and for seasons, and for direction, and navigation. The fourth Gift of the Spirit is teaching. The lights in the sky have helped us to always find north, so we were taught how to travel around without getting lost, and we were taught when to plant the crops, and when to harvest them, and when to go hunting, and when to have festivals and celebrations unto the Lord for all His goodness unto us. We were also taught just how big the universe really is, and how old, and how fascinatingly mysterious and complex, and yet so extremely consistent throughout its entire expanse. God's Laws cover a large territory.

In the fifth Day of Creation, God made all the birds and fishes, and commanded them to fill the seas and the sky. A very large percentage of all human nutrition comes directly from birds and fishes, and has ever since the flood of Noah. How thoughtful and generous of our Father to provide all the generations of man with a wonderful, and bountiful, and delicious, food supply. It is a supply of food that covers the whole earth, and never runs out, and is easily affordable for almost all people. The fifth of the Gifts of the Spirit is giving, and that corresponds perfectly with the fifth Day of Creation, when God gave us so much good food.

In the sixth Day of Creation, Father made the beasts of the earth. In that Day He also made mankind. He gave Man leadership, responsibility, and dominion over all the works of His Hands; over the fish, and the birds, and the beasts, and over all the earth, and all that is in it. Father set Man in the garden to tend it, and to name the animals, and to be fruitful, and multiply, and to fill the earth, and subdue it. The sixth Gift of the Spirit is leadership, or authority, and it is obvious how that matches up with the sixth Day of Creation.

In the seventh Day of Creation, Father rested from all His mighty works, and saw all that He had made, and it was good. God took a moment to evaluate all that He had so far done, and He liked it. He did not rest because He was tired. He rested because He was finished. There was no further need to create anything more, He already had made everything He wanted and needed, and everything we needed and wanted, too. It is admittedly difficult for me to perceive the direct link between the seventh Day of Creation, and the seventh Gift of the Spirit, which is showing mercy, or forgiveness. We know that God did not need to show mercy to Himself, since He never does anything wrong. As we understand the sequence of events, no one else had ever done anything wrong, either, at least, not yet. So why is the seventh day, Saturday, to be forever kept as a special and holy Sabbath unto the Lord, throughout all our generations? A day of rest from our worldly labors and pursuits, a day to read scripture, pray, rest, and remember the goodness of God?

Maybe the answer is to be found in part because God sees the end from the beginning. Of course He knew we were going to mess it up, so He wanted us to have the Sabbath to recall His mercy unto us. The High Sabbath of the Passover is certainly about mercy. So is the Yom

Kippur Sabbath. These are the most notable of all the Hebrew feasts and festivals. Therefore not only the weekly Sabbath, but also the high Sabbaths of the year are all about mercy.

So, perhaps the core purpose for all the Sabbaths is to remember to thank our God for His mercy, and to remind ourselves often that He could have easily killed us all for being so evil, and then He would not have had to become a human, and go be tortured to death, naked, in public, on a cross.

These things still remain mysteries to me. I can at this stage of my development only very dimly perceive the great Jewel of Truth, but I do know He's there, still alive, all-powerful, and He still knows I love Him, though I certainly do not understand Him.

THE NINE-LASER HOLOGRAM OF HEAVEN

Very obviously, there is a direct correlation between the numbers we find in scripture, and the structure of creation. We are also told that certain numbers are of special significance, among which are one, two, three, four, seven, nine, eleven, twelve, fourteen, twenty-one, twenty-four, forty, forty-two, fifty, seventy-two, and also, a thousand. Scientists and mathematicians will also mention things like pi and the largest prime number. For this experiment, we shall consider particularly one, three, and nine.

In the scripture, we are commanded to hear: "The Lord our God is ONE!" We are informed that all things proceed forth from Him, and all things are subject unto Him. We know that God will call all creation before Him one day to give an account, each creature personally, for every single thought, word, and deed we have done in this world, even if no one else but God ever knew about it. Personally, I do not have a speech prepared to present to Him. I imagine that I will be way too terrified to say anything, but, if possible, I will try to at least think something like, "I was wrong, about very many of the times when I thought myself correct. Please forgive me, because of Jesus, and, not for my sake, but for Your Holy Name's sake, try not to have me thrown into the lake of fire!"

Anyway, God is ONE, and the source of all, and also, God is ONE, and the destination of all. God has also proven in His Word, and with many miracles in this present world, to be the entire Holy Trinity, and has manifested His interaction in our lives as Father, Son, and Holy Spirit. The aspects of this concept are explored also in another story in this collection, namely, Length, Width,

WHEN LIGHT BECAME A MAN

and Depth. Simple math will tell us that three times three is nine, and the place we find a corresponding number is in the nine fruits of the spirit, namely, love, joy, peace, patience, kindness, goodness, faithfulness, gentleness, and self-control. Why three times three, to represent the attributes of God? Remember, God is always alive, throughout all eternity, always in the extreme past, always in the present, and always in the most distant future, even after the Day of Judgment. He informs us that He does, indeed, fill all of Heaven and earth, and that also includes all of time, too. Wouldn't you agree that He's a very large person, then?

At any rate, that provides us with two points of creative projection from God, into the nothingness, which He is continually doing, to hold all of creation glued together. One point of creative projection is the Beginning, and the other point is therefore the End. The Creator Himself forms the giant bookends of all creation. Jesus forms the bookmark. From each projection point in time, God streams forth His creation with three super enormous invisible laser beams, since God is LIGHT, and coherent light, at that, which means that every single wave is timed in perfect rhythm with all of its' fellow light waves. This is why a coherent beam can travel extraordinarily far without scattering, and can carry precise information, even numbers and codes for things, and can easily be made powerful enough to burn through steel plates. Okay, now you can see the two projectors, both actually the same God, from the beginning, one going forward in time to start, and the other coming here, backward from Judgment Day, to finish, from different points in time, and you can also see the three giant laser beams, Blue for the Father, Red for the Son, and Green for the Holy Spirit. As the beams stream out, they stream at an angle apart from each other, so one can tell they are separated into discreet colors. They form a shape like a giant three sided pyramid, or tetrahedron. The two pyramids have their bases touching, where the projection from the start passes into and through the projection from the end, forming patterns of interference. The steadily forward-moving intersection of the six beams, plus their three interference patterns, gives a total of nine beams. The overall superstructure must resemble a gigantic, three colored, three-dimensional Star of David. Where the beams meet and cross, solid matter is formed. This is possible because the main beams are LIGHT, but that LIGHT is more solid than any solid matter in the universe, though our eyes and telescopes cannot perceive it.

The first projection point is corresponding to the Father, and the ending projection point in the future is corresponding to the Holy Spirit. The intersection of the two projectors corresponds to the Son of God, corresponding to this present world, where He lived, and died, and lived again.

When I returned from Southeast Asia, and the troubles we had there, I went to school at the University of North Texas. As fine arts photography major, I studied a lot about light and optics. I even took a course in the physics department, where we worked with lasers and learned how to make a hologram, a three dimensional image. When one holds a hologram and rotates it, one can see the entire three-dimensional target rotate also in space, so one can turn it around and see how the back side of the object appears. This is something we were doing in 1975 and 1976, when I first came back to stateside. If mankind can take a single, one-color laser, and figure out how to turn it into a three dimensional photograph, is there any possible way to understand what God is doing with His giant nine-beam laser projection? If it ever will be understood by mankind, it will have to be because God patiently explains it all to us, with charts and diagrams, and even then, I do not suppose we will ever be able to more than dimly comprehend most of it. If there is to be any deeper comprehension of matters such as these, perhaps we can find the real answers by study of the scriptures, and prayer, and meditation. After all, the greatest scientific minds of all time were all Christians, something the scientists who are atheists, I call them Darwinists, would never want you to find out. Newton was a Christian, as was Bacon, as was a very long list which includes most of the major scientific discoverers since the dark ages. In fact, these days many scientists are becoming converted to Christianity, as science proves that what was recorded in the Word of God was totally accurate, and has always been. Modern science still cannot even answer all the questions that God asked of Job, during his interview with Him, when God quizzed Job about the various aspects of creation, and Job was properly humbled, because he could not answer God. That interview happened about five thousand years ago, and so-called science still would flunk God's test. Wisdom and understanding come only from God, so, if you want to know something worth knowing, get out your Bible, and get to know God. The Bible says that God and His Word are ONE, so, to know Him and love Him, start knowing and obeying His Word. Since God and His Word are ONE, you cannot claim that you love God, if you do not love and obey His Word.

As far as the manifestations of the fruits of the Spirit, we can easily see that the Father certainly has already shown us overwhelming love, joy, and peace. Just think about the Garden of Eden. Without any doubt, the Son of God showed us unequalled patience, kindness, and goodness. Anyone who is a Christian has only been allowed, or even able, to become Christian because the Holy Spirit shows us faithfulness, gentleness, and self-control. No one in this world is able to actually manifest self-control, unless the Holy Spirit strengthens the person to be able to perform with self-control. People in the world who say they can control themselves are liars, and they eventually give in to their urges, whether anger, lust, greed, or whatever. The Holy Spirit gives us self-control by changing the desires in our hearts, to want new, and much cleaner, and better, things for ourselves and our loved ones.

Now, you can begin to perceive the wonderful way in which God uses light to shape and mold and hold all of creation, just the way He wants it. Quantum physicists will tell us that light is precisely the construction material of all solid matter, even at the most sub-atomic level. I do wonder why He set a speed limit on light, though. Perhaps it is to continually remind us that He also set a limit on time, and that there is not much time left.

A final thought about holograms is this: if you take a hologram, and cut it, or break it, depending upon the material, into several smaller pieces, every single piece will still show the entire image, in three dimensions, of the original target, though the size of the images will be scaled down because of the smaller size of the fragment. God's Word tells us that we are fearfully and wonderfully made, and made in God's Own Image. How does it feel to realize that you, my friend, are a walking, talking, living, breathing hologram, made in the Image of Almighty God? Scared? Yeah, so am I. I told you He's very large. We are just some of the little fragments. I still find comfort in this: even the smallest fragment will still contain the entire image. By the time He's finished on Judgment Day, anyone of us left around with Him will most certainly be conformed to His Image, or we will already have been dispatched to the lake of fire. We'd better thank Him for it, since no one can do it for themselves.

THE GREAT ATTRACTOR

The two scientists were taking a much needed coffee break, and discussing some of the newest theories which they contemplated. They were both extremely sincere Christian gentlemen, who also loved the scientific quest to further understand God's magnificent Creation.

"Levity? You mean, like, humor? Jokes?"

"No, no. Levity is the name for the force that is the exact opposite of gravity. The ancient Greeks thought that it existed, but could not find proof at ground level, though they suspected that the planets and stars were somehow held up by it. At any rate, we now know, for the last few years, that the Universe is still expanding, and even accelerating faster outward all the time."

"True. So?"

"We've all been trying to guess what is pulling it outward with such force, since the initial thrust from the Big Bang would, of course, be a single shot."

"Continue."

"Maybe the answer has been staring us in the face all the time. Think about tidal force. The Earth's moon is tidally locked to the Earth, not the Sun, so the far side always faces away from the Earth. Why, since the Earth is so much closer, and apparently bigger, does the moon not orbit only the Earth? Because, despite the strange appearance to the contrary, the major player in the gravity game in the Solar System, from the moon's point of view, will always be the Sun, with something like over 98 % of all the mass in the Solar System. Each individual component within the gravity well of the Sun will respond most to the Sun, far more than any other planet. This is even true of the moons of the gas giants, as far removed from the Sun as they are. It applies even on a smaller scale, as in the asteroid belt. The bigger the concentration of mass, the farther reaching will be the tidal effects on the entire system overall."

"Field theory, on a grand scale? Okay, go on."

"As far as we know, the same dynamics apply on even grander scales, like the now verified central black hole in the middle of each galaxy. The one in the Milky Way has about four million solar masses. Andromeda has one fifty times larger than that, and will slam into our own Milky Way in about two and a half billion more years. The concentration of mass in every central black hole is what, through tidal forces, keeps the entire galaxy spinning as a single cohesive unit, instead of all the different pieces moving at different rates of speed. The huge spiral galaxies, which are the biggest by far, fly through space like gigantic frisbees, held together by the glue of tidal force."

"Okay, so tidal effect holds large structures together, so that they move and behave as though all the components are a single mass structure. How does that stretch out the sky, please?"

"Tidal effect also will stretch out something caught in an extremely strong gravitational field. If you fell feet first into a black hole, the two meter difference between the effect of intense gravity upon your feet versus your head would literally pull you apart, stretching you out like salt water taffy."

"All right, so tidal force stretches things out. Everything would still be falling inward into the hole, though, not stretching out like the sky is doing."

"Correct. That is, in a stable system, with no change in the mass of the source, or the intensity of the gravitational field."

"The only way the mass of a black hole changes, is when it eats another star, or, with the really big ones, maybe another galaxy."

"Correct again. You do know, however, that they never stop eating. They just sometimes slow down a little while, until they can pull in some more fresh meat. Every single one of them will eat however much you shove into it, and just keep getting heavier, and expanding its' radius and event horizon. It also continues increasing its' gravitational field, which, as it does so, reaches OUTWARD further and further!"

"OH!!! I SEE!!! The Attractor?"

"Correct again! The Great Attractor is where over 97 % of the entire mass of the whole Universe is concentrated at a single point in space. We know it probably first formed as a sort of space curve echo of the Big Bang, like a collapsing inward mirror image of the outward shockwave of the Bang, and is probably located in space about where the Bang occurred, where Father said

'LIGHT!' At any rate, we can measure that the Great Attractor is certainly the gravitational center of the entire Universe, and also that the tidal forces which it exerts are quite beyond human comprehension, but they certainly saturate and stretch throughout the length, width, and depth of the Universe, and it provides the fundamental gravity skeleton upon which the entire superstructure of the sky is suspended. The tidal forces from the Great Attractor are what are pulling the mass of the Universe outward, always faster, since every time the Attractor eats another galaxy, or cluster of galaxies, or even super cluster of galaxies, it grows, becomes more massive, and shoves its' tidal forces ever further outward, pulling the rest of Creation along behind it. The acceleration is still increasing also because there is no resistance in totally empty space, so the initial outward blast is only acquiring more velocity as the tidal forces are added to it. Not to worry; we will probably never expand faster than the speed of light, or the sky could seem to go dark, since the light from distant stars could never go fast enough to get back to us. Not only that, but, as space contracts, or curves, time slows. As space expands, time accelerates. Not only is space growing bigger and bigger, faster and faster, all the time, time is also going faster and faster all the time. Have you checked your watch lately?"

"It's time for an aspirin. You're giving me a headache."

"Sorry. I've had one since about three o'clock this morning, when I woke up from that dream where I saw all of this stuff in a flash."

For a moment, silence held. Then the dreamer said, "That's not all. This morning, I also think that the physical aspects, with which we are familiar, such as energy, time, space, matter, gravity, levity, and so forth, are representations of things in the unseen parts of creation, beyond the lenses of our telescopes and microscopes and x-rays. Energy may correspond to God's power, time may correspond to His eternal nature, space may correspond to His infinity, and matter may correspond to His solidity and reality. Gravity may be the physical representation of God's love. It has no upper limit, it is always attractive, and everything in Creation is subject to its' strength. It cannot be defeated, conquered, or ever nullified. Also, I think that the Great Attractor may be the unseen location of the Throne of God. Jesus said that if He were lifted up, He would draw all men to Him."

After a few seconds' thought, the friend asked, "To what, then, does levity correspond?"

The dreamer smiled, and said, "It represents the fact that He's not yet finished building. He's still the Creator, and He's still continuing to create new things. Levity corresponds to His creativity!"

AT THE END OF THE DAY

Ever since the beginning of time, there have been some very long days. We are not sure how long the Creation Days of Genesis lasted, since no one was around with a calendar or watch back then, except for Almighty God, and we certainly cannot tell how long a day is for God. I would never want to be someone stupid enough to say that a day for God has to be only twenty four hours, no more, no less. It never proves wise to try to limit God, or squeeze Him down into our little, tiny boxes, within which our thoughts usually remain. Just because our minds are limited, that can never limit Him.

But, since Day Six of Creation Week, the day He made man, we have a recorded history of things that happened in our own years and centuries upon the earth. The most accurate historical record

ever assembled is the Holy Bible. We
know that Abraham faced a long day,
indeed, the day God told him to sacrifice
Isaac. We do also know that the son of
Isaac, Jacob, faced at least one very long
night, when he wrestled all night with the
angel of the Lord. Who can even
comprehend how long the days were for
Joseph, while he was a slave, and later, a
prisoner, in Egypt?

When Moses led the children of Israel
out into the desert, one of the longest of
those long days must have been the day
the Lord parted the Sea and led them to
safety. As long as it must have been for
the Israelites, it was probably much
worse for Pharaoh, and all the drowning
Egyptians.

We are told of another very long day
for Moses, who, remember, was eighty
years old when God sent him to
challenge Pharaoh. One time, during a
big battle, the army of Israel was winning
the battle, as long as Moses' arms were

uplifted in prayer. As the day wore on, Moses' arms became tired, and whenever the arms dropped, the Amalekites started to win. To overcome this, Aaron, and also Hur, one on each side, held Moses' arms up, until the battle was over at sundown, and Israel had won.

Later in time, when the Hebrew leader was Joshua, there was a great battle to be won, as the children of Israel fought to claim their land. The five kings of the Amorites had banded together with anyone else they could enlist, and came to fight against a place called Gibeon, which had made a peace treaty with Joshua. Gibeon called for help, and Joshua brought the army of Israel up into the mountains by night, and they surprised the Amorite armies, and began to destroy them. As the battle wore on, Joshua realized that he would run out of daylight before he could chase them all down, and finish killing them. He prayed to God, and then, in faith, commanded the sun to hold still in the sky overhead, which it obediently did, for about the space of a day. This gave the Israelites the extra time they needed to finish the nasty job, and also proved that God was truly fighting for Israel that day.

There is little doubt that the longest day which ever occurred was approximately April 3, 33A.D. This is, as near as we can pinpoint, the Day of the Cross. That was a long Day for God as Father, God as Son, and God as Holy Spirit. It was also hellishly long for all the disciples, and the mother of Jesus, and anyone else who had met Him and loved Him. The amazing thing is that anyone at all could restrain His anger, and not quit halfway through, and then choose to not go ahead and destroy the whole world. He did that while He was being tortured to death, by the very people He had come to save. I could never do that, could you?

The one common element in all these exceedingly long days was this: God was there all day long, working, and, when necessary, fighting, for His people. At the end of the day, in every case, the Lord won the war, and gave the spoils of victory freely to His children, as though they had really won them for themselves. By doing these things God not only assured the survival, and even prosperity, of His people, He also, and of greatest import, brought Himself the Holy Glory, which it is, indeed, His right to have.

CROWN OF LIGHT

Suddenly, they found themselves standing on a large, flat, level plain, which stretched beyond the eye's limit, outward, on three sides. Although the open sky above their heads showed the brilliant stars in full splendor, there was no sign of the Sun, the moon, or even the Earth. The entire area was lit softly with a warm golden glow, which seemed to come both from the flat surface upon which they were standing, and also the air right around them. They were perfectly comfortable, with the temperature, pressure, and humidity so well adjusted to each person's personal preferences, that no one of them noticed even the slightest discomfort. Everyone noticed that his or her own body was completely whole and well, entirely pain-free, and strong, in perfect condition, and everyone began to smile, as they started to realize just how terrific all of this stuff had become, all within the first ten seconds.

Everybody began to notice the people around them, and every close family member, and every other Christian they had ever known, could be seen in the faces in the crowd. A muted, but excited buzz of conversation began, and quickly swelled to a happy roar, with some folks shouting over distance to other people in the crowd, who were some of their other buddies and friends. All of the good animals that ever lived were there, too. Everyone only dimly remembered the events of his or her own death out of the earth. The memories of all of that life were starting to fade, like someone waking up to a wonderful morning, after a long, restless night, tormented by nightmares and fevers.

Almost as one person, they suddenly began to notice that there was a safety line off to the right, along what seemed to be the edge of the gigantic surface upon which all the millions of them were standing. Beyond the safety lines, which seemed to be like steel cables, held by steel posts, up to about five feet tall, the view was of open space. Under normal conditions, this sight alone would have sent most people running for the hills, but for some strange reason, no one in the whole crowd felt anything but surprise and curiosity. Some began to wonder just exactly what kind of floating giant platform in outer space this thing would prove to be, and why only one side seemed to have an edge or limit, or any kind of safety lines. The more scientific minded wondered where the air, light, and gravity were coming from, and why it was not about three degrees absolute above zero. Most folks were just so joyous to be alive again, and with their loved ones again, that they were not even much noticing the other things around them.

A few of the sharper-eyed people in the group began to perceive another platform, off in the dark distance to the extreme right. In the vast darkness of the night sky, it had not been so easy to spot the other platform, with the thin, edge-on view that was what they were able to see from here. As their eyes adjusted to the dim light, they could make out other people there, but the whole place was very dark. The people over there were not happy to see each other, since they found themselves among old, deadly enemies, some of whom they had murdered, and some others who had done other murders. All the evil animals that ever lived were there, also. Unlike the first group, these monsters were not celebrating, but already fighting, cursing, screaming, and trying vainly to kill each other all over again. One could just barely hear the faint roar of angry fools, once again inventing warfare. They were all doing it at a very hand-to-hand level this time, too.

The distance between the platforms was maybe about a half a mile, so each side could just make out the details of the other people's platform. The people on the lighted platform were shocked and troubled a bit by the behavior of the savages across the gulf, but, as before, without fear, they were mostly saddened, and only for a moment at that, as they realized just how blessed each of them was, to not have been placed over on the bad side. In contrast, the people across the way were trying vainly to find a way to cross the gulf and come do harm to the good people, or, for some, to just escape the other monsters on the platform with them. There was no safety rail in place on the other platform, and, in some cases, losing balance, and, in some cases, being pushed, some of the folks from the bad platform fell over the edge, and screamed as they began to fall into the void.

Without warning, a very bright point of light appeared ahead in the night sky.

For some reason, the mind wanted to call it north of where everyone was suspended in space. It was slightly off to the right, for the people on the good platform, and slightly off to the left, for the people on the bad platform. Everybody froze at once and stared transfixed as the point of light grew rapidly into a roughly triangular shape, then into a throne, with a Man Who glowed like white-hot molten iron seated upon the throne. The spectacle continued to grow, impossibly large, so that the mind began to reel, as He continued to move closer. One would think He was already so large, that He could approach no closer, without smashing into them. He was taller than heaven itself, and His white wings stretched beyond the edges of the sky. His hair and beard were whiter than snow. As He moved ever closer, every single person, good or bad, fell on his or her face, trembling, but wanting, with terrified fascination, to take a peek,

and not miss something, like a kid at a
horror movie. As He came forward, all of
reality shook, and the universe quaked,
and the night sky began to roll back away
from Him, as curtains being drawn back
by unseen hands, and everything was
brilliant light behind Him, but He still
out-shined everything else.

When He arrived, He did not come
alone. At His left hand, there were three
mighty, terrifying cherubs, who were
Eden-el, Gabriel, and Michael. Following
right behind the cherubs were millions of
angels, all beautiful and terrible to see.

At His right hand, there were several
hundred thousand of His children,
resurrected in power and glory
resembling His Own. They also had
snow-white hair, and the men all had
long, full, snow-white beards, and long,
snow-white hair, but, all of them, like the
King, had faces of young adults, full of
knowledge and strength. Every one of
them, like the King, shined with a bright

white glow from head to toe. They each also had enormous, beautiful wings, and every child of light looked strong enough to crush an entire army single-handedly, and in reality, they could. Even the extraordinarily powerful cherubs would have been no match for any one of them. These were the ones which had been murdered for testifying, no matter what, that they would rather die, believing in the Son of God, than live a lie without Him.

The King had eyes like giant lasers, which seemed to burn white-hot holes right through you. No matter where He was looking, nothing could hide from His sight. His expression was very calm, and He even had a slight smile, and a thoughtful aspect. Whenever He looked directly at anyone, that person froze in place instantly, unless He commanded them to speak or relax.

He was wrapped in a glowing robe, woven from the top throughout, of one piece, without seams, which reached down to His glowing feet, as He sat upon His Great White Throne. The robe appeared as made of tightly woven threads, which glowed, with the intense colors of pure blue, red, and green, until one looked for a few seconds, and realized the impossible, that the threads of the fabric were actually beams of laser-like light, smoothly curving and conforming to the contours of His body as though made of cloth.

The scepter in His right hand did indeed appear as though a Rod of Iron, but as of white-hot molten iron, that still remained solid and held its' shape. At the top end of the scepter was a giant jewel formed of intense light beams, blue, red, and green. The jewel was essentially two base-to-base tetrahedrons, with the bases passed about halfway through each other, so that the entire object seemed to form a three dimensional Star of David. It rotated slowly, a slight distance from the end of the bar, always remaining exactly in the same spot in reference to the bar, as though held by some invisible solid link.

As stunning as all those things were, the most spectacular item of His apparel was His Crown. Similar in a way unto the robe, it, too, appeared as made of tightly wound beams of blue, red, and green light. It was shaped to resemble a crown that He had once worn, that had been made of thorns. The giant beams of laser were miraculously curved around each other in a type of basket-weave pattern that some enemy soldiers had used before when they twisted the thorns into a mock crown for Him. Woven into the braids of light were twenty one very brilliant stars, all nearly as bright as His Face. Each one was for one of the points of the thorns that had been jammed into His scalp. They were real, physical stars, each one many times brighter and much more massive than earth's sun, and they all burned an intense blue-white light out in all directions.

As His approach suddenly stopped, everything became perfectly still. No one and nothing moved or spoke, for about a half an hour, except everyone was quietly breathing, but not moving, otherwise, while they waited nervously to hear what He had to say. During this time each person experienced their own personal life review, and somehow they saw, and heard, the sum total of every single life experience, and memory, including every thought, word, and deed, and also, every other person they had ever met in their whole lives, all the way back to birth.

After this, He opened His mighty mouth, and said, with a great voice that resembled the sound of a great waterfall, but millions of times louder, "Stand up!"

Immediately, everyone, and everything, stood up straight, eyes wide with terror of Him.

WHEN LIGHT BECAME A MAN

As His eyes swept over all creation
before Him, He said, "This is the
moment, at last. I have many things to
say. First, I AM JESUS!"

When He said this, every single knee
of every single creature bent, and, as one,
they bowed their heads before Him.

Then He said, "Now, what do you
have to say about Jesus?"

Instantly, every single voice of every
single living thing, both good and evil,
shouted as though all one voice, saying,
"Jesus is God! Jesus is God! Jesus is
God!"

After a couple of minutes, He turned to
the cherubs, and said, "Bring forth the
enemy."

Suddenly, Michael reached his hand
into a sort of hole in the fabric of the sky,
and pulled an ugly thing out of the hole, a
grotesque, misshapen thing, warped by
its' own evil into a sickness for the eyes
and mind to see. No one really wanted to
look at it, but justice had to be served

before witnesses. Michael held it as it struggled, easily holding it in one hand, while he wrapped a great golden, unbreakable chain around the dragon, then wrapped its hands and feet in something that resembled barbed wire, which were the iniquities it had knowingly committed. So, it was finally bound forever, both with the chain of justice unto death, and with the cords of its' own iniquities unto punishment. Michael, Gabriel, and Eden-el dragged it before the throne, as it still struggled, uselessly.

The King looked down on the beast, and said, "I told you I was going to kill you for starting all this stuff. Your death starts today. Since you were the first to do evil, and the last to stop it, so will be your time in the lake of fire. You will be the first one in, and the last one out. Remember My cross? The only way out of that was My death, and that's the only way out of the fire for you. I will not torture anyone forever, but you will repay, in full, all the pain and suffering you ever caused. Now keep your mouth shut, you've already lied enough, and I do not want to hear your screams as you die. Be gone!"

As the King said the last word, the enemy was suddenly yanked away from Him, and began to fall, dropping between the two giant platforms, where the humans all were watching, and the ones on the good platform were shouting praise to God and cheering as the devil fell into the Lake of Fire, which had miraculously appeared below the gap between the platforms. The devil fell faster and further than the humans which had fallen or been pushed off of the evil platform, just a few seconds before. As the thing landed in the Lake of Fire, a huge splash of liquid flame leapt upward, and crashed back down, covering the dragon. It immediately caught on fire, and began to writhe silently, in unimaginable agony.

Instantly after this, the King commanded the evil angels brought before Him, and all the good angels did so, binding every single demon in chains of justice. They were promptly dispatched, also to the Lake of Fire.

Next, the Lord Jesus said, "As I said in the Beginning, 'Let Us make man in Our Own Image!'"

Immediately all the good angels flew down to the platform full of evil humans and animals, and began to throw them over the edge into the Lake of Fire. The evil animals were vainly trying to bite and claw the good angels, but it was hopeless. The evil humans also tried uselessly to fight the good angels, or run from them, but again, to no avail. In about fifteen minutes, most of the evil humans and animals had been removed. At this point, the King said, "Finish it!"

Instantly, the three cherubs, each one himself larger than a planet, raced in a straight line to the far side of the large platform of the evil creatures, and reaching down with both mighty arms, they each grabbed the platform's edge, and began to lift. All the good angels also came over to the same edge, and also helped lift. The entire mammoth platform, larger than a continent, which had been holding billions of human beings, and trillions of animals, including all evil bacteria and viruses, began to tilt toward the Lake of Fire. The people and animals on the good platform watched silently, and not even the good animals made a sound, as all of their old enemies were sent to die. At last, the cherubs and the angels threw also the whole platform itself into the huge Lake of Fire.

The King reached down to the Lake of Fire with one hand, and scooping it up into His mighty fingers, He shoved it into another gigantic hole in the fabric of time and space, and, withdrawing His great hand, empty, He said to the hole, "You shall close now, and you shall never open again." The great rip in time and space slammed silently shut, and disappeared.

All the good angels, and the good cherubs, as well as the children of light, began to fly toward the people and animals on the remaining platform, everyone greeting old friends and acquaintances. As they merged together, the platform itself was expanding, growing larger and larger. The entire sky became light, and there was no more darkness anywhere, only areas of less intense light, here and there. The platform turned green under their feet, and grass and other plants began to sprout and grow tall with what resembled the speed of a time-lapse film from the old world. People found all their old pets in the huge, noisy crowd of happiness, and not a single one was missing.

The King gently cleared His throat, and everyone stopped a moment, and turned to look at Him, and waited to hear His Word.

"The reason you are still with Me, and not gone with the others, all of whom We will now forget, is because of this: You heard what I told you, and you did it. That is exactly what I wanted. Now, you blessed, enter into the joy of your Lord, prepared for you before the foundation of the world!"

As He said this, a great, white, shining City descended from the uppermost part of heaven, and came to rest upon the new earth, which continued to expand the whole time. By this time, many fruit trees had already grown to full size, and were bearing ripe fruit, perfect, and delicious. Among all the trees, there was one special tree, which had descended with the Holy City of New Jerusalem, and had been in the Garden, hidden within the massive walls ever since the beginning of time. As the Tree of Life began to grow ever larger, and spread out mighty branches, and bear much fresh fruit, the King smiled, and said, "I think it is time now for you to finally eat the fruit of the Tree of Life. All sin is forever removed, and now you can all live together with Me, without any possibility of sin ever again."

The river of the Water of Life was flowing out from the base of the Throne, and all the resurrected people began to come to the Tree, and to drink from the River. The memories of sin, evil, pain, and sorrow were already fading from each person's mind, except for the Lord. He had already forgotten it.

As He walked among His people upon the new earth, in His scaled down, but still almighty, human body, giving and receiving warm smiles, and lots of handshakes and hugs from everyone, and kisses, too, from the little girls and puppy dogs, He had to smile as He thought back on it all. A long, very long, and tough, very tough indeed, project, but it was still all worth it when it was over. Now He had achieved everything He had wanted, and all of His people would now share in it with Him, forever. He was scheduled to go fishing with the apostles and Paul later on this afternoon. As He watched one of the children learning to fly with his new wings, slamming into a tree, but laughing it off, and trying again, He chuckled to Himself. The apostles would never suspect that He was going to spike the place where they were going to fish later today with about a trillion extra fish, just to make them all laugh. In His first lifetime, He could never afford to tell even one joke, or ever be anything but life-and-death serious. His mission just had not allowed for that at all. Things were different, now. They were finally going to get to see His wonderful sense of humor, too.

JESUS FREES US

Jesus is our Master, and He saves us from disaster.

Jesus is our Lord, and He keeps us moving forward.

Jesus is our Savior, and He changes our behavior.

Jesus loves the meek, and improves the way we speak.

Jesus hates the proud, and no arrogance is allowed.

Jesus kills the cruel; He demands the golden rule.

Jesus loves the kind, and purifies the mind.

Jesus is really God, and that isn't really odd.

Jesus is our Friend, who fights beside us till the end.

Jesus is our God and King, and He created everything.

Jesus our life indeed protects, with never any big neglects.
Jesus is His Majesty, Jesus Christ has set us FREE!!!

SPARK IN THE DARK

Kindle a candle in the name of the
Lord;
Raise hands in praise; keep moving
forward.
Follow the path He reveals unto you,
And always remember, His Word is
still true!
Do not follow your heart; it will lead
you astray,
But study His Word, and hear, and
obey!
Let the love of the Most High
transform your heart,
You'll be happier at the end, than
you were at the start.
Stay humble and honest, as His Spirit
decrees,
Always honor the Lord, if His soul
you would please;
Do goodness to others, expecting no
thanks,

And store up your treasures in
Heavenly banks.

THE GOLDEN EAGLE

I saw a very strange thing yesterday,
about midday. As I was returning home
from running an errand, I was walking up
my front walk, and I heard the raw voice
of a raven or a crow, coming from the
south, and I thought it might be in the
trees in my back yard. It sounded again,
louder. Then, in a second, a mighty,
huge, golden bird, floating with
motionless, outstretched wings, glided
silently into view from behind the trees,
about 200 feet up. Chasing him were two
crows, trying to pick at his tail feathers.
They squawked again, and then tried to
move in close. This time the eagle
sounded that beautiful and unique
piercing cry, and abruptly changed
course, just as he arrived right overhead
of me. He headed east, toward Jerusalem,
and flapped his great wings twice, to
accelerate and leave the nuisances

behind. It was almost as if he did not really want to hurt them. The extremely foolish pests would not let it go, but squawked again, and flapped as hard as they could to try to close with the giant bird. This time he did not say anything, but in the blink of an eye, he turned and reached out his mighty talon, and grabbed one of the birds. He held it for less than a second, and seemed to fling it lightly away from him, as one would toss an empty cup into the trash can. The instantly dead bird fell motionless from the sky. The eagle continued on his eastward course, but the remaining bird was last seen flapping furiously to try to catch the eagle again, since after the quick kill, the eagle had slowly flapped his 6-foot wings about three times, and climbed much higher, with little effort. They vanished eastward behind the trees.

Do not seek trouble, but do not let it stop you, either. Finish your mission. That's why you were made.

THE HONOR RESERVED FOR HIS FRIENDS

How much better I, than the starry
midnight sky,
To sing our Maker's praise, than the
sunset's golden rays?
And how much finer me, than the
creatures in the sea,
To tell the truth about our King, though I
am also a created thing?
More fitting for a child of man,
mountains cannot, but, yes, we can
Give thanks and glory to our Maker
More fully than the ocean's breaker,
And though they are all within His reach,
Do the sand grains praise Him from the
beach?
Nor can the clouds in the sky above
Wonder at the mystery of His love.
For, though He made them all: it's true.
He died on the cross for me and you.

And His plan was always, from start to
end,
To make someone who would be His
friend.

THE LORD IS ONE

In the Name of the Father, the Son, and
the Holy Spirit:
Father, hallowed is Your Name.
Your Kingdom come, Jesus;
Your will be done, Holy Spirit; as in
Heaven, so in Earth.
Father, give us this day our daily bread.
Jesus, forgive us our sins, for we also
forgive our debtors.
Holy Spirit, lead us not into temptation;
instead, deliver us from evil.
For Yours is the Kingdom, Jesus, and
Yours is the Power, Holy Spirit, and
Yours is the Glory, forever, Father!
Amen.

ABOUT THE AUTHOR

We could spend a lot of time talking about my life, or we can better use the time learning about the life, death, and resurrection of Jesus Christ. The most important things anyone ever needs to know about me are these:

I believe in God the Father Almighty, Maker of Heaven and Earth, and in Jesus Christ, His Only Begotten Son, our Lord, Who was conceived by the Holy Ghost, born of the Virgin Mary, suffered under Pontius Pilate, was crucified, dead, and buried. He descended into hell. The third day, He rose again from the dead, and ascended into Heaven, where He is seated at the right hand of the Father. From thence, He shall come to judge the quick and the dead. I believe in the Holy Ghost, the Holy Church, the communion of saints, the forgiveness of sins, the resurrection of the body, and the life everlasting.

BACK-JACKET TEXT

Did you ever wonder if there was something hidden in plain sight in the Word of God? God's mind is far above our minds, and we can never fully understand all of His Ways. No matter how many times you read God's Word, you always continue to find new insights. (As we mature and grow, our wisdom changes.)

Dive headfirst into this experiment! Do not fear new, strange concepts, if they do not contradict God's Word. Search out hidden treasures of wisdom, pray for the Lord to guide your search, and see if you might discover things no one else did!

Check your Bible for confirmation of these ideas. Try to imagine what it would be like, to be there in person, watching Him work miracles!